Luke wasn't interested in Jeris.

She was an okay woman, but she wasn't in his ballpark. He was sure something would have clicked between them by now if a relationship was meant to be. But he'd felt nothing when he'd seen her, even if it was only a few times.

Why would Audra try to push her on him? Maybe Jeris was in league *with* Audra. Maybe she'd put Audra up to this. Now he felt more than chagrined. He jerked open his car door.

Brady clambered out of the backseat and shut his door. "Hurry, Dad. Let's go fishing."

Luke got out slowly. "Remember? We're eating first. Then we'll go fishing. I'm sure Audra has the food on the table by now. Or almost."

"Aw—"

"Watch your manners, son. And no begging during dinner. When we've finished eating, I'll take you outside. You can't go outside alone because of the water. You understand?"

"Yes, sir."

Brady ran to the front door.

Luke trudged toward the door as if he were going to a root canal. As he passed Jeris's SUV, he thought about what he would face inside the house. A sticky wicket? A good description. It would be awkward and definitely *not* relaxing as he'd first thought when Audra invited him and Brady for the afternoon. Because Jeris would be there.

Well, he would show Audra. And Jeris. He would be polite to her. But that was all.

KRISTY DYKES, a former newspaper columnist, is an award-winning author of nine Christian fiction titles as well as over six hundred articles in many publications including two New York Times subsidiaries. She was voted to the 2004 Heartsong Presents Favorite New Authors List, and her titles have been on the Christian bestsellers list and the Top 20 List at christianbook.com. Her novella, "Reunited," in *Wedded Bliss?* won third place in the 2006 Book of the Year Contest, contemporary novella category, presented by American Christian Fiction Writers. Kristy writes a column for the e-zine of FHL, the inspirational chapter of Romance Writers of America. She's taught at many conferences and two colleges and enjoys speaking for women's and writers' events. She and her husband, Milton, a pastor, live in Florida. She loves hearing from her readers: kristydykes@aol.com or www.christianlovestories. blogspot.com

Books by Kristy Dykes

HEARTSONG PRESENTS
HP564—The Tender Heart

The Heart of the Matter

Kristy Dykes

Heartsong Presents

To my hero husband, Milton, who is my collaborator in the deepest sense of the word—he's believed in me, supported me, and cheered me on in my calling to inspirational writing.

Thank you, Emmett and Sonja, for all the times you've entertained us at your lovely home on the water. It was the inspiration for the setting of this novel. And when you shared with me the pictures you captured of your glorious double sunset over the water—as well as your toothbrushing manatee—well, I got all tingly and knew I had to include them in the novel.

A note from the Author:
I love to hear from my readers! You may correspond with me by writing:

Kristy Dykes
Author Relations
PO Box 721
Uhrichsville, OH 44683

ISBN 978-1-59789-428-9

THE HEART OF THE MATTER

Scripture quotations are taken from the King James Version of the Bible.

Scripture quotations are taken from the HOLY BIBLE, NEW INTERNATIONAL VERSION®. NIV®. Copyright © 1973, 1978, 1984 by International Bible Society. Used by permission of Zondervan. All rights reserved.

All of the characters and events in this book are fictitious. Any resemblance to actual persons, living or dead, or to actual events is purely coincidental.

Our mission is to publish and distribute inspirational products offering exceptional value and biblical encouragement to the masses.

one

"I want everybody to pray that God will give me a mommy," little Brady said in a heart-tugging, grown-up way.

Luke Moore took a deep gulp as he sat in the church pew and stared at his six-year-old son—the boy who'd just made the prayer request.

Giggles and guffaws rippled across the sanctuary.

Luke felt the hair on the back of his neck rising. Was every eye on him and Brady? With a quick look around at the mostly elderly congregation, he noted nearly everyone was staring at them.

"I want everybody to pray real hard." Brady stood on tiptoes, clutching the pew in front of him, looking earnestly at Pastor Hughes behind the pulpit.

Luke stretched his long legs out in front of him and traced the crease in his crisply pressed suit pants. *Brady should be in a children's program this morning,* he thought with a rueful pang, *if only there were one.* In all the time he'd attended this church, he'd never seen a child give a prayer request in the Sunday morning service. Would the parishioners be offended by Brady's antics?

Luke glanced about the sanctuary, looking for the usual two or three children who regularly attended the church. But he saw only one child this morning. His son.

And my son is now throwing a paper airplane across several rows of empty pews!

"Psst, Brady," he whispered. "Sit down." He tried to keep the irritation out of his voice. No telling what might happen next.

"Don't be a doubting Thomas," Brady sang out in perfect

pitch, his unruly blond hair a cross between Dennis the Menace's and Opie Taylor's from the old *Andy Griffith Show* reruns, one of Brady's favorite TV programs. "Trust fully in His promise," he sang. "Why worry, worry, worry, worry—when you can pray?"

A tidal wave of deep chuckles and bright laughter swept through the congregation.

Pastor Hughes attempted to restore order, then gave up. He was laughing too hard.

Luke drew a sigh of relief as Brady finally plopped down on the pew. The tyke glanced up at him, looking as pleased as a peacock, his giant smile revealing a missing front tooth. Luke's heart warmed to the boy.

"Brady wants a mommy," Pastor Hughes said good-naturedly from the pulpit. His face took on a serious look. "Folks, never discount a little one's simple faith. In fact, the Lord Himself instructed us to come to Him with childlike trust for our needs. Let's bow our heads and do just that. Let's go to the Lord with childlike faith. Brother Jernigan, will you stand and lead us to the Lord in prayer?"

An elderly man rose slowly to his feet. "Father God, Almighty Lord in heaven, we come to Thee with surrendered hearts. . . ."

Luke closed his eyes and tried to concentrate on Brother Jernigan's prayer. But he couldn't. He was thinking about what Brady had said. *A mommy.*

It was as if Luke weren't sitting on a padded pew in Christ Church in Silver Bay, Florida. Instead it was several years ago, and his wife, Sarah, was telling him about a young woman she'd met at church that morning. . . .

❧

"My heart goes out to this girl," Sarah had said as they drove home from church. "She has a three-year-old son she's giving up for adoption." Her eyes misted with tears.

Luke swallowed hard, feeling her pain. The greatest desire

of Sarah's heart was to have a child. But that would never happen. A doctor's recent diagnosis had confirmed it.

"The girl is a good mother apparently, but she got pregnant young—at fifteen—and she's only eighteen now. . .and. . .well, she feels this is the right thing to do, to give up her son. She's looking for a Christian couple who wants to adopt."

Luke realized he was gripping the steering wheel as if he were having a blowout. He forced himself to relax his hands. But he couldn't relax his inner quakings. He knew what this was leading to, what Sarah might ask.

"Luke. . ."

He kept his eyes on the road, wondering what Sarah would say next. She knew their agreement. They'd made a pact never to bring up the subject of adoption again. They'd reached that conclusion after two adoptions had fallen through and the pain was simply too great to bear. For her. For him. He wanted a child, too.

Sarah reached across the car and touched his arm. "I always wanted *your* child, Luke. One who looked just like you. I wanted him or her to have dark brown hair and dancing eyes like yours. And I wanted him to have a strong sense of what's right, just like you do." Her voice broke. "I. . .we both know. . . that can't happen. At least not in the way we expected it to. But after hearing the girl's story this morning, I'm wondering if God is about to drop a blond-haired, freckle-faced boy into our laps. He's so cute. Just wait till you see him."

Within months he and Sarah had signed the papers and joyfully welcomed Brady into their home as their son. Sarah, especially, had been in heaven.

Two years later she really *was* in heaven. She'd passed away from a fast-growing cancer.

&

Lord, Luke prayed, *give me the strength and wisdom for the momentous task You've called me to do—to raise a son by myself, at least for the time being.*

Brady pulled on Luke's coat sleeve. "You can open your eyes, Dad," he chirped in his loud, high-pitched voice for all to hear. "Brother Jernigan said 'amen' a long time ago."

Luke felt his neck burning, but he smiled. *Little boys can certainly keep life interesting.*

Pastor Hughes read the scriptures, then began preaching.

Luke pulled a pen and notepad out of his coat pocket and handed them to Brady, hoping they would keep him occupied. As the pastor talked about temples and trumpets, Luke's mind wandered again as he thought about his many conversations with well-meaning friends.

"When are you going to start dating?" they frequently asked. "You need a wife, and Brady needs a mother."

Luke couldn't disagree with them. What they said was true. Trouble was, there was no one in the church to date, at least no one who interested him. He knew he probably wouldn't find a cover-girl, perfect wife like Sarah, but he wanted whomever he married to be attractive and stylish. In his line of work, a financial advisor at Gulf State Bank, he had to attend and host numerous events—parties, banquets, gala affairs, and more—with the elite of society.

Sarah had always loved attending those functions with him, dressed in feminine after-five attire and promenading by his side, making him proud. She'd been the diamond among the rhinestones with her keen sense of style and her unparalleled beauty. She'd even won him a few clients with her charming, amusing ways.

"Why can't you find a wife?" a friend wondered. "You go to plenty of social events. Women are all around you, if only you'd look."

His friends were right. To a degree. For instance, last evening he'd attended a dinner party in a client's home. Among the twenty or so guests, two single women were there. One even flirted with him, pretty brazenly, he thought. But he'd shied away. To his way of thinking, the only women who made good wives were church women—dedicated Christians. Trouble was, all the women he knew at Christ Church were married—or old enough to be his mother or grandmother. So forget that.

"Why don't you change churches?" another friend suggested.

No way. When they'd moved to Silver Bay, the town Sarah grew up in, they'd chosen to join her home church from childhood. Several years ago Luke had been elected to a deacon's position, and he would be loyal to Christ Church no matter what.

"Then why don't you attend some singles' groups in other churches? Surely you can meet someone at one of those. Large churches have lots of singles' events."

Right again. Only he didn't have time to go traipsing all over, scouting out women. Maybe when Brady was older. But not now. Fatherhood was demanding with a capital *D*. And so was his job. How would he find baby-sitters for Brady if he were to go on numerous dates? He could barely find them for his business engagements. Mrs. Nelms, the elderly woman who'd baby-sat twice last week—and many times in the last six months—had recently made it clear that she wasn't finding enough time for her own grandchildren. Last night, for the dinner party he'd gone to, she'd turned him down, and only after several frantic attempts had he found a sitter.

"I repeat, Luke," Pastor Hughes said from the pulpit. "Will you stand and close our service in prayer?"

Luke shot to his feet, smoothed his trousers, fumbled with the buttons of his navy suit coat.

"Dear ones," Pastor Hughes said to the congregation, "shall we bow our heads as Luke leads us to the Lord in prayer?"

Luke led in prayer—shakily—feeling guilty that his mind had wandered during the sermon. When he came to the close of his prayer, he said a respectful "Amen," turned around, and gathered his notepad and pen. "Brady, it's time to go."

"Yippee!"

"Son—" One glance at little Brady, and Luke was squelching a big smile.

"Oh, I forgot." Pastor Hughes leaned into the microphone on the pulpit. "Folks, I really do have a good memory." He touched his graying temples. "It's just short." He burst out into big chuckles. "We have one more thing to do before we go. Everyone, please sit down. I want to introduce you to someone."

The congregation took their seats.

"I'd like for Dr. Jeris Waldron to come to the pulpit. She has a special announcement to make."

Luke heard a slight noise behind him, turned, and saw Jeris Waldron stand up. She was the woman he'd met a few weeks ago after morning worship. Pastor Hughes had introduced them in the church foyer. He'd sat by her during Sunday school a couple of times. Luke hadn't noticed she was sitting in the pew behind him this morning.

Absently he watched as she made her way to the front of the sanctuary. He pushed in the button on his ballpoint pen. In, out, in, out. A few moments ago he'd been thinking there weren't any women of marriageable age in the church. Of course. Jeris Waldron was of marriageable age. But she didn't meet the criteria he had for a wife. He noticed her bland appearance—very little makeup, an ugly black oversized jacket, and a black skirt that was too long. And with no jewelry, it was apparent she didn't know how to accessorize. Last Sunday she'd worn a gray outfit like the one she had on today.

A gray persona. He winced, feeling bad that his honest assessment was so critical. But it seemed to fit her perfectly.

"I believe some of you have met Jeris," Pastor Hughes said. "She recently joined our church. She's a child psychologist and is starting a new practice here in Silver Bay. Jeris is the daughter of a former parishioner in Winter Haven whom my wife and I knew when we pastored there years ago. She was like a daughter to us when she was growing up. When we found out she moved here, we went to see her and asked her to join Christ Church. To our delight she did. Now we've convinced her to accept a new undertaking. She's going to tell you about it." He took a seat to the right of the pulpit.

Jeris crossed the platform, placed a notebook on the pulpit, and adjusted the microphone to her mouth. "Thank you, Pastor Hughes. I'm happy to be a member of Christ Church." For several moments she bragged on Pastor and Mrs. Hughes, how fine they were as pastors, how much they loved their parishioners, and how she had received that love beginning when she was a child.

She cleared her throat and opened her notebook. "I'm pleased to tell everyone I'll soon be starting a children's church program during the morning worship service."

Polite murmurs could be heard from the members of the congregation.

That's wonderful, Luke almost said out loud. He figured Jeris Waldron would be great with kids. She would probably apply her vast knowledge of psychobabble to teaching them, and that would be a good thing.

"Brady, that's your new children's church teacher," Luke whispered.

Brady was drawing circles on four different offering envelopes. He didn't look up but kept drawing.

"I have big plans for the children's church program." Jeris's voice dripped with enthusiasm, and her face lit up. "First of all, I'd like to see it grow. If any of you have grandchildren or know of children who aren't attending church elsewhere, I'd like to find out about them. I intend to make home visits and tell people about our program. Please write down the names and addresses of any children you may know and turn them in to me."

Luke heard whispers. He glanced around and saw pleased expressions on people's faces.

"Second, I'm planning some exciting events for the children. Parties, puppet shows, picnics, and more. This will not only attract new children but it will also minister to the children we now have. If you get a call asking for assistance in chaperoning or for other duties, I hope you'll be willing to help out.

"Third, and most important, I'm doing this for a purpose; and that purpose is to win souls—children's souls—to Christ. Statistics show that most people who are living for the Lord were won to Christ when they were children. It's important for us to provide a climate in this church where young hearts can be influenced for God."

She leaned into the pulpit, probably for emphasis. "It's been said that a man asked the famous minister of yesteryear, D. L. Moody, how many people got saved in his revival meeting on a particular night. Moody told the man two and a half. The man said, 'You mean two adults and one child?' Moody said, 'No, two children and one adult.' The man was surprised, but Moody explained that children were just as important to the Lord as adults. Moody went on to say that when children give their hearts to the Lord, they have their entire lives to work for Christ; but when adults get saved, they have very little time left to devote to Him."

The church members applauded.

Luke clapped, too, but he was fuzzy about what he was applauding for—some minister from yesteryear? Charging through his brain were the myriad things that awaited him at the office tomorrow.

Maybe I should get some work done this afternoon.

He bit his bottom lip, engrossed in his thoughts. When he tuned back in to the pulpit goings-on, Jeris Waldron was filling in the details of her strategy for her children's church program.

Of course he was happy about her plans. Clearly the program would benefit Brady, and that was a pleasant, even welcoming, thought. He'd be taught the Bible on his level during the morning worship service. No more paper airplanes sailing across the sanctuary. And no more prayer requests about a mommy.

But Luke hoped he wouldn't be called on to assist with class parties and picnics. He didn't have a minute to spare.

Even for such a worthy cause.

two

Jeris looked across the dining room table at Pastor Hughes and his wife. She was enjoying spending time with them in their parsonage and discussing her plans for the new children's church program. Pastor Hughes was telling a preacher joke, and she and Audra Darling were laughing.

The pastor's wife would always be Audra Darling to Jeris, what she'd told Jeris to call her as a child. It had to do with a Southern thing, Jeris mused. The Hugheses were originally from Alabama. It also had to do with the fact that Audra wanted to be called something special by children, and all children called her this endearing name.

Jeris smiled as she thought about how Audra Darling pronounced her name. It came out as a Southern *Au–dra Dah–lin'*. Jeris smiled again, thinking she was probably the only adult who called her Audra Darling. But that was okay with her. It spoke of the bond between them.

"Thank you for a delicious dinner," Jeris said. "Again." This was the second time they'd invited her for dinner since her move to Silver Bay.

"You're mighty welcome, Jeris." Pastor Hughes drained his iced tea glass and set it on the table. "You have a standing invitation."

Jeris flashed them a big smile. "Do you know what that means to a single woman who's just moved to a new town and doesn't know a soul?"

"It means you can come over anytime you want," Audra Darling said. "Isn't that right, Andrew?"

Pastor Hughes nodded vigorously.

Audra Darling stood, picked up Jeris's plate, and raked the

scraps onto her own plate. "In fact, we expect you to." She picked up her husband's plate and did the same. "You're a grown-up version of the fine little girl we used to know when we pastored the church you grew up in, and we're looking forward to some good times with you now that you've moved to Silver Bay."

Jeris felt moisture forming in her eyes as she recalled happy times spent with the Hugheses. They'd never had children of their own, and they'd been almost like a second set of parents to Jeris. She had loved them that much.

Age-wise they were the same as her parents. But physically they were nothing alike. Her dad was short. Pastor Hughes had a commanding presence with his over six-foot height. And her mother was the exact opposite of Audra Darling in the looks department. Where her mother was a jeans-and-T-shirt-type woman, Audra Darling was elegant with her sophisticated clothing and highlighted hairstyles that changed every few months.

Jeris looked over at her now, noticed her bright red manicure that matched her striking red suit, heard the jangle of her silver charm bracelet as she reached for a serving bowl, and pictured the red high heels she was wearing that showcased a red pedicure.

The phone rang.

"Excuse me a moment." Pastor Hughes reached behind him and picked up a phone on the buffet, then stood, gestured toward the family room, and left.

"Isn't it interesting how life turns out?" Jeris handed her salad plate to Audra Darling. "Who knew way back then I'd be working in a town you two happened to be pastoring in?"

"God." Audra Darling's gaze was piercing, as if it could read Jeris's thoughts.

Jeris nodded. Audra Darling could be depended on to assess a person or a situation, and she no doubt was discerning this situation correctly—that God had brought Jeris to Silver Bay.

Jeris had prayed for God's guidance before choosing the town to start her practice in, and she believed He had guided her.

"He's got His reasons for bringing you here. And He'll let you know in the by-and-by." Audra Darling chuckled. "And I don't mean in the *sweet* by-and-by either."

Jeris laughed at her reference to the afterlife.

"The Bible says our steps are ordered by the Lord." Audra Darling scraped the salad plates and stacked them.

"I memorized that verse as a child."

"And our stops are, too, as D. L. Moody once said."

"I've never heard that quote. That's pretty good."

Audra Darling wagged her head. "We've had several stops in our ministry, times when the Lord led us to move on to take another pastorate in a different town."

"I'm glad He led you here and that you were willing to come." Jeris envisioned Christ Church. Though the congregation was small and the buildings old, she had confidence the Hugheses would see growth once they'd been here awhile. They'd moved to Silver Bay only months before Jeris did. "I'm glad He led me here, too."

"We love the people. And Silver Bay. I believe we'll be here until we retire. We have big hopes and dreams for the church's future."

"Then I'll be able to sit under your ministry for at least—what? Ten more years? Isn't Pastor Hughes fifty-five now, as my dad is?"

Audra Darling nodded. "And maybe we'll stay a year or two beyond that."

"That's great to hear. Twelve more years with you as my pastors."

"Nothing could please us more." Audra Darling flashed her a brilliant smile. "Maybe when you're married and have children, your kids'll look at Andrew and me as another set of grandparents."

My kids? What a pleasant thought. Jeris had counseled lots of children and had a special connection with them. She looked forward to the day when she had kids of her own. On second thought, perhaps she should say *if*. The years were ticking by fast.

"I'm praying God will send you a fine Christian man, Jeris."

Jeris was at a loss for words. She certainly hoped the same thing. But what could she say? No men were on the horizon, not even within radar range.

Audra Darling picked up the stack of dishes and made her way toward the kitchen. "I'll be back in a jiffy with our dessert."

"May I help?" Jeris stood.

"No." Audra Darling waved her back down. "Sit tight. Won't take me but a minute. You might like looking through the church pictorial directory. It's on the buffet. It'll help you put the names with the faces of our members. It helped me when we moved here."

"That's a good idea." Jeris reached over and picked up the directory, her thoughts on the Hugheses as pastors. She flipped through the booklet, looking at each picture, reading each name. Every church the Hugheses had pastored had grown under their leadership. And, more important, their parishioners had been nurtured and spiritually fed. Everybody loved them.

She remembered when they'd moved away from Winter Haven and how sad the church folks had been to see them go, her family included. She was sixteen at the time, and they'd promised to come back for her high school graduation, which they did.

When Jeris married at twenty, Pastor Hughes performed the ceremony, something she'd planned on since she was a child. He also conducted Jeris's husband's funeral three years later. That was a long time ago—nine years. Now her life had meaning and purpose in her profession as a child psychologist. That was what she focused on these days.

Audra Darling came back into the dining room, carrying a

tray with a layer cake on one end and cups and plates on the other. She set it on the table, poured coffee into a cup, and held it out to Jeris. "You take cream? Sugar? Sweetener?"

"Cream." Jeris took the cup and poured cream into it. "Thanks."

Just then Pastor Hughes hurried into the dining room. "I have to get to the hospital."

Audra Darling put her hand over her heart. "Is it Brother Ward?" She turned to Jeris. "He's in the last stages of congestive heart failure and has complications. Diabetes, too. They've given him less than three months to live. He's only in his forties." She shook her head. "Did he—"

"No. As far as I know, he's still okay. This call came from Sister Sloan's daughter. Her mother tripped on a throw rug, and they're rushing her to the ER. She may have broken her hip, and you know what that means. Surgery, usually."

"Poor Sister Sloan." Audra Darling looked at Jeris again, concern etched in her features. "She's a charter member of Christ Church. She's ninety-seven and has dementia." She turned back to her husband. "Do you think she's strong enough to come through it?"

"I don't know. But I *do* know she—and her family—need our prayers."

"Do you want me to go with you?"

"No need to. You stay here and visit with Jeris. I'll call you after I find out the prognosis." He kissed his wife. "But don't look to hear from me for several hours. You know how emergency rooms are. See you." He said good-bye to Jeris and left.

Jeris marveled at what had just transpired. To be cared for by such a fine pastor and his wife was a blessed state, in Jeris's opinion. And she welcomed being cared for. She'd spent the last decade earning several degrees and had taken no time for herself or anyone else. Studying and applying herself to her chosen field had been her way of life. Now she was being pulled into the warmth and loving care of the Hugheses. And the thought was music to her ears.

Audra Darling sat down. "Mind if we pray for Sister Sloan before we eat our dessert?"

"Oh, let's do. Sounds like she's going to need it."

Audra Darling reached for Jeris's hand and led in prayer. When she finished praying, she sliced the cake and handed Jeris a piece.

For more than an hour they chatted about Audra Darling's cake recipe, the church, the ministry, Silver Bay, Audra Darling's interests, and more.

The conversation turned to Jeris, her move to Silver Bay, her interests, and then to her new practice.

"What made you want to become a psychologist, Jeris?"

Jeris smiled, thinking about the twists and turns of life that sometimes propelled one to follow a certain course.

"When you started college, wasn't education your major? Wasn't that what you told us you were going to study when we asked you at your graduation party?"

Jeris nodded, remembering the festive occasion. "I wasn't sure what I wanted to be."

"Like many graduating seniors."

"I thought teaching would be a good thing."

"But you quit college two years later to get married."

"Wesley and I fell in love when I was seventeen. When I turned twenty, he said, "Why wait?" After all, he was twenty-six and had already graduated from college. He was eager to get married."

Audra Darling placed her hand over Jeris's. "And then you had only three years together as husband and wife. Sometimes life is hard to understand. Who would have thought he'd die so soon?"

Jeris nodded soberly, remembering the exact moment she'd received the news of the small plane accident that took her husband's life.

"My heart went out to Wesley the first time I saw him. He was just a boy—maybe six or seven years old—and he was climbing down from that great big church bus." Audra Darling rubbed the rim of her coffee cup, her gaze fixed on the glass-fronted china cabinet across the room. "His home life. . .it was so. . .tragic. An alcoholic father. . .a mother who didn't have enough backbone to. . .to protect her little ones from his meanness." She swallowed. "We tried to help him. And his family, too. We tried so hard."

"You did a lot for them. Wesley always said that. Through yours and Pastor Hughes's help, he and his family had good things to eat and clothes to wear. And he came to know Christ. That's the most important thing of all."

"When you called and told me you were marrying him, I'll have to admit I couldn't picture you two together." She paused. "Your backgrounds were so different." Her voice was almost a whisper. "I wish—" She stopped abruptly. Silence hung in the air. "He. . .he was a good Christian boy."

He was a product of his upbringing. Jeris took a sip of her coffee, now cold.

"He died so young." Audra Darling shook her head, her brows drawn together. "Knowing what Wesley went through in childhood, was that what propelled you into the field of psychology? You saw what he experienced, and now you want to help others?"

Knowing Wesley propelled me into the field of psychology. Period.

❧

After a pleasant afternoon with Audra Darling, Jeris felt glowingly good as she drove home, despite the overcast sky. The woman had a way of bringing sunshine into any situation, it seemed. They'd chatted and laughed like girlfriends who were the same age, not like what they really were—one old enough to be the other one's mother. Audra Darling was fun, but she was spiritually refreshing, too.

A gentle January rain started, and Jeris flicked on her windshield wipers. Recalling a TV weather report, she slowed down. The weatherman said the first few minutes of rain were as prone to cause accidents in Florida as snowstorms up North because of hydroplaning. The water mixed with the oil on the streets and became as slick as glass, causing a car to slide sideways and possibly wreck. Only when the streets were thoroughly wet did the risk of accidents decrease, the weatherman said.

I sure don't want to hydroplane. On this road. Or in my life.

Now that she'd started her own practice, she was excited about what lay ahead. She wanted to set a steady course on what would bring her fulfillment and happiness and not get sidetracked.

In the professional arena, she hoped to become a well-respected child psychologist in Silver Bay with a thriving practice. She ached for children with deep-seated needs and would work hard to help them.

In spiritual matters she wanted to serve the Lord and put Him first. She'd done that since she was a child and would continue. She looked forward to teaching children's church and influencing little lives for God.

She had financial goals, too. She hoped to earn enough money to own a home and take pleasant vacations. She had a good car and a nice apartment, but owning a home would give her a sense of permanency and roots. And vacations would give her rest and relaxation so she could come back refueled and refreshed.

She also desired to make new friends in social settings. She'd always been on the shy side, and friendships had come hard for her. But she planned to reach out more, to show herself friendly, as the Bible put it. And having the dazzling Audra Darling as her mentor, she felt certain of success.

The rain increased, and she turned her wipers on high speed.

Whop-whop, whop-whop, whop-whop, the wipers droned. Combined with the driving rain hitting the car, the noise was enough to drown out her thoughts for a moment.

Good, because the only other area of my life I can think of is romance, and I'm not sure about that.

Romance? She'd had that once. Or at least what she thought was romance. At seventeen, who knew what anything was, especially love? She'd been fooled. Wesley's attentiveness, affection, and tender ways when they dated turned into domination, jealousy, and control as soon as they walked up the aisle.

"The last time I fell in love, I was seventeen years old and as naive as a newborn," she whispered, as if to summon up strength for the determination forming in her heart. "The next time I give my heart away, I won't be as foolish. A good-looking man will *not* sway me."

Movie-star handsome, Wesley had constantly belittled her after marriage. He'd humiliated her for everything, it seemed, particularly her plain-Jane appearance and lack of education. She couldn't seem to find her way careerwise, and he took delight in pressing that upon her at every opportunity. She'd tried several jobs, but nothing worked out. She'd felt worthless. According to Wesley, she wouldn't know how to put fries in the grease at a fast-food restaurant.

With tears and a hurting heart she would try to talk to him about his attacks and tell him he couldn't keep treating her that way. But he would tell her he didn't know what she was talking about, then berate *her* for her audacity to bring up such awful accusations against *him*.

She didn't know then that he was a product of his up-bringing, as she'd thought when listening to Audra Darling today. She didn't have a clue why he treated her the way he did. The only thing she knew was to cry out to God and ask Him to give her a strong, faithful love for Wesley.

And God did. He answered her prayers. She determined

she would stay true to Wesley because she'd made a vow before God and man, as her grandmother used to put it. And she determined to love him, no matter what.

To try to please Wesley, she'd enrolled in college again. Perhaps something would click for her and she would find her career path. One of the first courses she took was psychology. During her first semester, she discovered why Wesley was the way he was.

Then he died. She grieved for him as if he'd been Prince Charming. She'd loved him with her heart, soul, mind, and strength; and she'd been more wounded at his death than in living with him, if that could be so. Only a person who'd walked in her shoes could understand that.

It was shortly after his death that she knew what she wanted to do. She would spend her life helping people understand what was happening to them and why they acted the way they did, particularly children. And then she would help them change their behavior.

Nine long years had passed since Wesley died. She was ready for a relationship and had been for some time. Like any woman, she wanted to love and be loved. But she was wiser now; she had more head knowledge and heart knowledge. She would be careful, as cautious as a kid on his first day of swimming lessons. She had decided she would be discerning in her choice, unlike last time.

The last few years, no one had come along for her. Her time clock was ticking. Would she go through the rest of her life single, as her aunt Betsy had?

"I would've married, if only the right man had knocked at my door," Aunt Betsy always said. "But he never did. So I just continued on my merry way. Did I say 'merry'?" she would add with a wry smile.

Jeris saw the windows fogging. She leaned toward the dashboard and turned on the defroster. *Is that how it'll be for me someday? Fifty-four years old like Aunt Betsy and not married?*

Her stomach knotted, and her heart pounded. She didn't want to go through life single and alone, without a man to care for her and her to care for him. She wanted a husband. And she wanted children. Two, maybe three.

Whop-whop, whop-whop, whop-whop.

Was that her heart or the wipers?

❧

Sitting at the kitchen table with her husband, Audra ate a bite of toast. She loved this time of day. They read the Bible and prayed together. After that, they read the newspaper, then began their busy day.

Andrew chuckled. "Listen to this." He described that day's installment of his favorite cartoon, the one about the couple who constantly locked horns in marital battles.

They both laughed.

Audra took a sip of coffee. "Listen to this." She read aloud each frame of the comic that featured the long-time single woman who'd finally found her man. "I wonder if Jeris follows this comic strip? It might give her hope that she'll find Mr. Right."

"Mr. Right?"

"I told her yesterday I'm praying for God to send her a husband. If ever a girl deserves a good man, it's Jeris." She paused as she looked out the bank of windows facing the water. "I can't wait to see her married and happy, with a houseful of children—"

"A houseful?"

"You know what I mean. Two. Several. Whatever she wants. She's going to make a great mother."

"Like you."

She thought of what Andrew had told her many times. He'd said that even though God didn't send them children, He had used her to minister to many women, and by doing that she'd become their spiritual mother.

"I'm glad Jeris moved here. I think one reason God sent her

is for you to be a friend to her, Audra."

She nodded. "I look forward to that. She's a neat young woman."

"And I believe the Lord is going to use you to lend your expertise to help her."

"Expertise?"

"Can you take her shopping?"

She knew exactly what he was talking about.

"She wears such old-looking clothes."

"They're expensive."

"I don't doubt that. Jeris has good taste. Unfortunately it doesn't manifest itself in her clothes."

"They're called travel knits."

"But nobody her age wears that stuff. You don't even wear things like that."

She looked down at her outfit. She was wearing a crisp white cotton blouse that had tiny tucks down the front and hung over her tiered brown gauzy skirt. She wore a bronze metallic belt low-slung at her hipline that matched her bronze metallic, high-heeled, open-toed shoes. It was the latest look, and she had several of the new tiered skirts. She could dress them up or down depending on the occasion. Put a fitted T with a tiered skirt and team them with raffia-beaded wedges, and she could go to a picnic, as she'd done yesterday. Today, for the church office, she'd chosen the dressier look with heels.

"Why don't you take her shopping and get her to buy some outfits like you're wearing? Or something similar?"

She thought about the bland colors Jeris wore and the sameness of the style. A gray knit suit. A black knit suit. A brown knit suit. A taupe knit suit.

"Why don't you two go to the new mall that just opened in Tampa? Take a whole Saturday and show her the ropes. Shop to your heart's content."

"And I could get some new outfits, too, huh?" She grinned at him.

He chuckled.

"I could take her to a cosmetic counter and let the girl give her a makeover. And maybe I could schedule an appointment at the hair salon so they could update her style."

"And please get her to buy some new shoes."

She laughed, envisioning Jeris's shoes. Like her knit suits, they were all the same. Closed-in loafers with short heels. And she nearly always wore black tights or black hose. "But I wouldn't want to offend her with any of this. I wouldn't want to risk hurting her feelings. She's too sweet a girl."

"She's a psychologist. Explain what you have in mind and the rationale behind it."

"That she should be wearing brighter, younger-looking clothing because she's young and has great skin and facial features and hair, and she should be showing them to their best advantage?"

He winked at her. "You're right on track." He wiped his mouth with his napkin, then stood up. "We need to get going."

"Andrew?" She looked up at him.

He glanced at his watch, then picked up his Bible, put it in his briefcase, and snapped it shut. "Yes?"

"Remember when I said I told Jeris I'm praying that God will send her a husband?"

"Yes, I do."

"I think Luke would be the perfect candidate."

"Don't tell me you're going to do some matchmaking between them." He set his briefcase on the floor and stood there looking at her, his eyebrows drawn together.

Audra playfully jutted her chin in the air. "It worked for Al and Gloria, didn't it?"

"I guess I can't deny that."

"And that's the only time I've ever tried matchmaking, you have to admit." She stood up and pushed her chair under the table.

"Right."

"You know I don't go around poking in other people's business."

"I've seen enough pastors' wives like that, and I'm mighty glad you're not one of them."

"But I definitely felt the leading of the Lord concerning Al and Gloria. All I did was point them in the right direction."

He laughed. "Toward each other. By inviting them both to dinner several times."

"It worked, didn't it?"

He pulled her to him in a big bear hug. "I think they're almost as happy as we are." He drew back and gave her a syrupy look, then grinned.

She smoothed his shirt placket, her mind still on Jeris and Luke. "Jeris needs a husband, and Luke needs a wife."

He nodded. "Luke *does* need a good woman in his life. He needs a special woman, what with having a son and all."

"Jeris could be that woman. In fact, she'd make an ideal wife for him."

"Anything's possible, I suppose."

"The Bible says, 'With God all things are possible.'" She laughed, but she was as serious as she'd ever been.

"True. Jeris is tops in my book. Luke couldn't get a better wife than her. Maybe it'll work out between them."

"I think they'd make a great couple."

"And you said you're praying about it, right?" He rolled his eyes, but he was smiling at her.

She smiled back. Brilliantly. "Sometimes prayers need legs." She pictured a prayer in a cartoon's dialogue cloud. Underneath was a set of legs. They were wearing bronze metallic, high-heeled, open-toed shoes.

three

Jeris turned on the portable CD player and smiled as the lively children's praise song filled her classroom. It was early, and she'd have plenty of time to get things ready.

She scanned the room, pleased with the work she'd accomplished this week. A low table in the center would seat eight or ten children—she had high expectations—for coloring and table games. And stations against the walls would provide a variety of activities—a dress-up area with Bible character costumes, a cozy reading circle complete with a rug and bean-bag chairs, a kitchen for the girls, a tool bench for the boys, a track with cars and trucks, and shelves holding building blocks.

She'd collected some things from classrooms that weren't being used. Other items she'd purchased. Besides the stations, the children would have plenty of space to prance around to the beat of the praise music during song time. She couldn't wait to see the classroom filled with activity.

How many children would show up this morning? Besides preparing the classroom in the evenings after work, she'd made calls and visits, trying to drum up some students. She felt sure Brady Moore would be here today. He was a regular. And the other two children who attended Christ Church. But she hoped she'd have at least a few more.

She made her way to the tall metal cabinet and pulled out several new boxes of crayons and two stacks of papers she'd photocopied from the master book. She walked over to the table in the center of the room, placed the crayons on it, and put a coloring sheet at each place.

"Dr. Waldron?"

She turned around when she heard a man call her name,

the second stack of papers still in her arms. She spotted Luke Moore and his little son, Brady, standing in the doorway. "Luke, Brady." She rushed over to the door and gave the child an exuberant hug. "Please come in, both of you." She released Brady and thrust out her arm toward the room. "Brady, I have some nice activities planned for you."

Brady stood as if transfixed by the wonderful things he saw.

"Brady," Luke said, "say, 'Thank you, Dr. Waldron.'"

"Jeris," she corrected. "I want the kids to call me Jeris." She tapped the tip of Brady's nose.

"How about *Miss* Jeris?" Luke said. "When I was growing up, I was always taught to address ladies like that."

"That's okay, too. All right, Brady, I'll be Miss Jeris. How about that?"

"Thank you, Miss Jeris." Brady dashed across the room. He stopped at the car track and pushed a tiny truck along the grooves. "Vroom, vroom, vroom."

"See you later, Brady," Luke said.

"Vroom, vroom, vroom."

Luke shrugged his shoulders at Brady's lack of response. "Looks as if he's going to enjoy your class, Ms. Waldron. Or is it *Dr.* Waldron?"

"I'm hoping all the children will enjoy our class. And it's Jeris." She extended her hand and gave his hand a firm shake.

"Well, I'll see you later. . .Jeris. I'll pick up Brady as soon as church is over." He rushed out of the room.

"No need to hurry," Jeris said into the air. She returned to the table and continued putting papers at each place.

She hadn't expected Luke to hang around as some parents might, either clingy parents or parents trying to soothe an unhappy child. She didn't expect Luke to stay ten minutes. Or even five. She didn't think he needed to make a big effort to get to know his son's new teacher. That wasn't important.

But she *did* expect him to stay a few minutes and talk about Brady. She knew Brady's background, of course, how he'd been adopted and Luke's wife had passed away. Audra Darling had told her that much. She expected Luke to ask a question or two about the new children's church program, maybe make some comments and perhaps tell her a few tidbits about Brady, his favorite activities, his spiritual training, and where he went to school.

But Luke Moore had bothered with none of that. He'd rushed out of her classroom—and away from her—like he was a fireman on the way to a fire.

She'd gotten his meaning loud and clear, hadn't she? She was a psychologist. She possessed an inner sense, a knowledge the average person was unaware of. She watched people's mannerisms and body language, their nuances, what they said—and didn't say, which was as important. She could read people like a book, as the saying went. Simple as that.

And she'd just read Luke Moore. In her opinion Luke Moore wasn't interested in Jeris Waldron, with his handsome good looks and his impeccable attire and his fabulous career. To him, she was too plain and too boring. She didn't have enough pizzazz or wit to attract him.

She put the last coloring sheet on the table, then walked over to the countertop and looked in the upper cabinet for the box of cookies she'd put there earlier.

Luke's sentiments were fine with her, because she felt the same way about him, only from a different angle. He was too handsome for her taste. And too full of himself. She was sure she would find that out when she had more interaction with him—no, *if* she did. He probably would remain aloof and no doubt had an ego as wide as the Gulf of Mexico, like most handsome men.

Give her a balding, bookish guy any day. They had no egos. Only tenderness, what her heart craved from a man.

❧

"Jeris?"

Grasping the box of cookies, Jeris turned and saw Audra

Darling at the door. She was pleased she'd stopped by. She motioned her in. "Come and see my classroom."

"I'd love to. You sure I won't hold you up from what you need to do?" She glanced down at her watch.

"It's still early yet. I have plenty of time before class starts."

Audra Darling made her way across the room and gave Jeris a motherly hug. Her gaze swept the area. "It's nice, Jeris, very nice."

"Thanks. I would've painted it, too, with Pastor Hughes's permission, of course. But I didn't have time." Jeris pointed out the various play stations.

"You did a fine job. The children will love it." Audra Darling looked over at Brady who was busy at the car track. "Come here, Brady Moore, and give me a hug." She smiled and held her arms out to the boy. He ran toward her, and she embraced him, their faces lit up by smiles.

Jeris reached down and caressed Brady's chin. "When'd you lose your tooth, Little Man?"

"Last year." He jumped on one foot, then the other, over and over.

Jeris laughed. "You mean last week or last month, don't you?" She knew most children his age had trouble judging time. And from the looks of his gum, the tooth had only recently come out. "Did you get some money under your pillow?"

He nodded vigorously, his eyes glowing like stars. Then he zoomed back to the car track and picked up two more cars.

"Isn't he darling?" Audra Darling stared after him.

Jeris smiled. Audra Darling loved the word *darling*. "That cute little freckled face will steal your heart." She watched him playing with the cars and trucks as he made his "vroom-vroom" sounds. Little Man would be her nickname for him. She liked it.

"You're looking for an assistant, aren't you?" Audra Darling's eyes twinkled.

"Yes. I have a teenage helper this morning. But I'd like an

adult on a permanent basis, and then, as the class grows, I plan to have a couple of teenage helpers every Sunday."

"Would you consider a woman the age of a grandma as your assistant?"

"You?" Jeris was surprised. Audra Darling had never mentioned the possibility.

"Well, you know how much I adore kids."

"Yes."

"And I'm experienced. I've taught all age levels in church work."

"Yes."

"And I have a deep desire to do it."

"Yes."

"And. . .I'd really like to work with you. At least for a while. Would that be okay with you?"

"Yes. Yes. Yes." Jeris laughed.

"I've led women's ministry ever since we've been here. But I just handed it over to a woman I believe will do a good job with it. So I'm free at the moment from ministry duties, and I'm ready to take on something else."

"When can you start?" Jeris laughed again. She was ready to sign her up. It would be a pleasure working closely with her. And she needed the help.

"How about right now?"

"That sounds great."

Audra Darling reached into a black canvas bag on her arm and pulled out a pink stuffed French poodle. The dog matched her tailored pink linen suit and her pink manicure. She barked like a dog and waggled the stuffed animal in the air. "I came prepared."

Brady came running. "Can I hold your doggie?" He jumped up and down in front of her.

"Only if you sit down. Fifi likes gentle petting. And she likes to sing. Want to hear her sing a song?"

Three more children dashed into the room, and Jeris found

herself occupied with the parents as she answered questions about the children's church program. All the while she noticed Audra Darling interacting with the children in the free play area and how they seemed to take to her and her to them.

Audra Darling played a significant part in my past, she thought. *Maybe she'll do that in my future.*

❧

Jeris spotted Luke as he walked into the classroom to pick up Brady. She made her way to him, as she planned to do to every parent, today and every Sunday. She wanted to greet each one and be available for any questions, maybe give them a recap of the Bible story she'd taught their children.

"How did Little Man do today?" Luke scanned the classroom. "There he is."

Jeris spotted Brady hammering an oversized plastic nail into a workbench. So Luke called him Little Man, too? She thought she'd found a private nickname for him.

"Did he miss me?"

She smiled. "To be truthful, no."

"Thanks a lot."

"What I mean is, we kept them pretty busy."

"I'm just kidding." He glanced around again. "From what I can see, it looks like you've created a place kids will be eager to come to every week."

"That's my goal. I did the same thing at my office, too." She thought about her waiting room—low tables with blocks, toys in a large chest, and a playhouse in the corner with working windows and doors. Her philosophy was to make a child feel comfortable and happy, and perhaps he would talk about what was bothering him.

"Brady," Luke called. "It's time to go."

"Let me get his coloring sheets." She walked to the nearby desk and found Brady's papers, then returned to Luke. "Here."

"Thanks." He folded the papers in half and stuck them in his Bible. "Brady, let's go."

Brady trudged over. "Aw, do we have to, Dad?"

Jeris leaned down to Brady's eye level and touched his cheek. "I have a treat for you, Brady. I have a treat for all the children since this is our first day of class."

Brady jumped up and down. "What is it? What is it?" His eyes were starry, like before, and his grin-with-the-missing-tooth was nearly as wide as his face.

"Normally the treasure box is reserved for—"

"The treasure box?" He jumped higher.

"Hold your horses, son," Luke said. "Let your teacher finish her sentence."

Brady kept jumping.

Jeris started again. "From now on, the treasure box will be for when you kids memorize your Bible verse or bring visitors. But today, since it's our first Sunday, I'm going to let everybody get a prize. Go look in it, Brady, and select anything you'd like."

"Yippee!" He raced away.

"Children, let me have your attention." Jeris turned toward the kids and gave instructions about the treats.

Bedlam broke out. The children saw Brady digging in the treasure box, and they all made a mad dash for it, toys flying in the various play stations and costumes left in heaps. Parents arrived, and by the time she'd delivered the correct coloring sheets—as well as the children—to the correct parents, she noticed Luke and Brady had slipped out.

I never had a chance to tell Luke about our Bible lesson on how to pray.

Into her mind popped the prayer request Brady had belted out last Sunday during the service.

"I want everybody to pray that God will give me a mommy."

&

"Luke!"

Luke turned around in the narrow hall of the church and saw the pastor's wife hurrying toward him. "Hi, Audra."

"Wait up," she called. "I need to ask you something."

"Sure." He leaned against the wall and watched Brady playing with his ball-on-a-paddle he'd gotten from Jeris's treasure box. "Brady, be careful with that thing. Don't hit anybody if they walk by."

"Yes, sir, Dad." Brady hit it into an open doorway, the ball going crazy on the end of the long elastic cord.

Audra reached Luke. "I saw you come into the children's church room and pick up Brady, but I was putting away the paints and paintbrushes and didn't get a chance to say hello."

"It was pretty busy in there."

"Which we're thrilled about. We had six children in class today. Jeris worked hard all week bringing in new students."

Luke nodded. That was good. Brady would meet some new friends at church. "So you'll be helping with the program?"

"Yes, I volunteered to be Jeris's assistant."

"You certainly love kids. . . ." He looked down at Brady, thinking how much his son liked Audra.

"I'm looking forward to working with them. And with Jeris."

"Pastor said you knew her when she was growing up?"

Audra told him they'd met Jeris when they were pastoring her home church in Winter Haven. "She's always been special to us."

"She seems to feel the same way about you."

Surprise etched Audra's face. "When have you two had time to talk? Have you been out or something?"

"No. I only met her at children's church."

"Of course. I didn't mean to presume."

He shrugged. "I just gathered it from all she said about you and Pastor Hughes from the pulpit last Sunday."

"Oh, that's right. When Andrew called her up to make her announcement?"

Luke nodded. "I figured you were pretty close."

"Can we get hamburgers and milkshakes for lunch today,

Dad?" Brady piped up. He stood statue still, his eyes imploring, his palms together in a prayer stance, his ball and paddle stuck in his back pocket.

Luke and Audra laughed.

"Please, Dad? I haven't had a hamburger since—"

"Night before last." Luke smiled, then felt his face growing warm. He didn't want Audra to think he didn't feed his son properly. "We eat out almost every night, but it's not hamburgers all the time. 'Course if Brady had his way we'd be at Jolly Hamburgers five nights a week. But most of the time we eat at Dale's Café. They offer a balanced meal."

"I don't have any hamburgers and milkshakes at my house"—Audra put her hand on Brady's shoulder—"but I have a roast in the oven and rice and gravy and—"

"I hope you're about to invite us to dinner." Luke chuckled, thinking about Audra's dining table laden with food, something he'd enjoyed a couple of times.

"Yes, I am. I'll have Sunday dinner on the table in a jiffy. Can you come?"

"Is the sky blue?" He smiled broadly. "Is grass green?"

Brady looked disappointed.

She caressed Brady behind the ear. "As I said, Brady, I don't have any hamburgers or milkshakes at my house. But Pastor Hughes said the fish were biting yesterday. It's been so warm lately. Maybe you can drop a line in the water and see if you can catch one."

"Yippee!"

"So I can expect you and Brady, Luke?"

"You can count on it. My mouth's already watering."

"Wonderful." She paused, looking contemplative. "I didn't even think to ask. Is it okay for Brady to go out on the dock with his Sunday clothes on? Last time I invited you I called in advance so you'd be prepared."

"It's fine. He'll have a blast. And I'll enjoy it, too. I've been needing to do something like this." He rubbed the back of his neck. "My work's been heavy lately."

"You're a hard worker, Luke."

He shrugged.

"Let's go, Dad." Brady tugged on Luke's suit coat. "I want to go catch some fishes at Audra Darling's house. Maybe if we catch some before she gets there, she'll cook them for us."

Luke laughed. "Well, we'll sure work at it, Little Man. But I think she said a roast is on the menu for today."

Audra shifted the chain of her purse to her other shoulder. "Maybe after we eat, we can all take a boat ride, like we did that other time."

"Yippee!"

"That'll be fun, won't it, Little Man?" Luke envisioned the warm sunshine and the sparkle it put on the surface of the water.

"Yes, sir."

Audra laughed at Brady's grown-up-sounding response. "You've trained him well."

"I work at it." Luke rubbed the top of Brady's head.

"It's evident what a good father you are, Luke." She looked down at her watch, her brows drawn together. "I'll be home in about twenty minutes or so. Unless Sister Sasser snags me in the foyer and tries to show me her scars from her latest surgery. This time it was gall bladder, and they did it by laparoscopy. She has scars here"—she poked at her stomach with a bright-pink fingernail that matched her pink suit—"and here"—she poked another place—"and here"—yet another. "She's apt to give us all the gory details next."

"Audra, you are a mess."

Her eyes twinkled with merriment. "Go on in the house when you get there. You know where I hide the spare key. Same place the last pastor hid it."

"Thanks. See you."

"And go on out to the dock if you like. Andrew left his tackle box and some cane poles on the back porch."

"It sounds so relaxing that I think we'll run by the house and change clothes."

"Then I'll probably beat you. I'll see you when you get there." She patted Brady's shoulder again. "See you, buddy."

"Yes, ma'am."

She smiled. "Your daddy's raising you to be a Southern gentleman through and through. He's a fine daddy." She turned back to Luke. "Oh, I invited Jeris Waldron to come, too. I wanted you to know."

four

After Luke and Brady changed clothes, Luke drove to the parsonage while Brady sat in the backseat busily engaged with a video game.

Luke's mouth was watering, as he'd told Audra. The woman was a first-class cook. She ought to write a cookbook—she was that good. He was looking forward to her roast and rice and gravy today. He could almost smell it cooking, that distinct roast beef scent. She'd entertained Brady and him last month and served roast then, too. The other time he'd been there, she'd served baked ham. But he could eat her roast every Sunday and never get tired of it. It beat Dale's Café's roast entrée all to pieces.

He wondered what she would serve for dessert today. Last time it was homemade chocolate cake and ice cream. He hoped she'd have the same—he could never get enough chocolate.

He turned onto Trout River Drive. The parsonage was in an older part of town on a body of water that flowed out to the bay. The church had owned the house for decades. But they'd kept it up, painting it through the years and making other improvements. A few months ago, after the Hugheses accepted the pastorate, the church replaced the kitchen cabinets, refinished the wood floors, and recarpeted the bedrooms, compliments of hard-working retired parishioners who'd put in long hours to get the refurbishing done.

As a board member, Luke had heartily approved the costs. He was glad they'd done it, for Audra's sake. A woman liked a well-kept home. Especially a woman like Audra. He knew it the moment he met her when the board interviewed them.

She was a class act, with her up-to-date clothing and hairstyle and her sparkling personality. If he married again he hoped he would find a woman like her, only younger, of course.

And he wanted to marry again.

He contemplated his situation.

"Predicament" was what his friend Ben called it.

"Double bind" was what his business colleague Paul dubbed it.

"Straits" was what his babysitter Mrs. Nelms labeled it.

"Sticky wicket" was how old Brother Jernigan put it.

It seemed he was the brunt of a lot of people's comments. And conversations. And that aggravated him. Why couldn't folks mind their own business? At work and at church he was frequently told that he, as a single man, needed a woman in his life in the worst possible way.

He pulled into the parsonage driveway, letting out a long, steadying breath. Deep down, he admitted to himself, what they said was true. He needed a woman, a wife who would love him and Brady. But he would never let anybody know how he felt. He didn't like talking about it. When the perfect woman came along, he'd make his move. Until then he'd have to wait. And people would, too. That was all there was to it.

As he drove down the long driveway toward the house, he saw Jeris Waldron's car parked close to the garage door. He knew it was hers because he'd seen her leave church in it last Sunday.

Nice. It was an expensive, late-model SUV. *At least you have good taste in cars, Jeris.*

He braked, then threw the gearshift into PARK with more force than was necessary. He knew exactly why Audra had invited Jeris today. He could add two and two—after all, he worked at a bank, didn't he? Audra must want to get the two of them together. People did things for a reason. And that was the reason Audra had extended an invitation to Jeris for Sunday dinner—when he and Brady would be there.

How convenient.

"Oh, I invited Jeris Waldron to come, too," Audra had said at the church. *"I wanted you to know."*

He wasn't interested in Jeris. She was an okay woman, but she wasn't in his ballpark. He was sure something would have clicked between them by now if a relationship was meant to be. But he'd felt nothing when he'd seen her, even if it was only a few times.

Why would Audra try to push her on him? Maybe Jeris was in league *with* Audra. Maybe she'd put Audra up to this. Now he felt more than chagrined. He jerked open his car door.

Brady clambered out of the backseat and shut his door. "Hurry, Dad. Let's go fishing."

Luke got out slowly. "Remember? We're eating first. Then we'll go fishing. I'm sure Audra has the food on the table by now. Or almost."

"Aw—"

"Watch your manners, son. And no begging during dinner. When we've finished eating, I'll take you outside. You can't go outside alone because of the water. You understand?"

"Yes, sir."

Brady ran to the front door.

Luke trudged toward the door as if he were going to a root canal. As he passed Jeris's SUV, he thought about what he would face inside the house. A sticky wicket? A good description. It would be awkward and definitely *not* relaxing as he'd first thought when Audra invited him and Brady for the afternoon. Because Jeris would be there.

Well, he would show Audra. And Jeris. He would be polite to her. But that was all.

❧

"Can we go fishing now, Dad?"

Luke looked down at Brady, pleased at how polite he'd been throughout the leisurely dinner. Audra and Pastor Hughes were superb hosts, and with Audra's cooking, a dinner party at their house was guaranteed to be enjoyable. Today had met his expectations and then some—but only because he'd kept a good distance between himself and Jeris. Just the way he intended for things to remain.

"Da—a—a—d, can we go fishing now?"

Luke took the last bite of his cake—chocolate, as he'd hoped—then wiped his mouth with his napkin. "Five more minutes, Little Man, okay?"

"Yes, sir."

Luke touched his midsection. "Audra, you did it again."

Audra looked across the table at him, smiling. "What?"

He gestured at the bowls on the table. "You scored a ten."

"Thanks, Luke. I love to cook."

"You should give cooking lessons." Jeris put her napkin beside her plate and settled back in her chair. "I, for one, could use some."

"I'll be the first one to sign up," Luke said. "All I know how to do is make toast and coffee. And soup and sandwiches." He paused. "Oh, yes, and cereal." He laughed. "Right, Brady?"

Brady threw him a crooked smile.

Everyone at the table laughed.

A shadow crossed Brady's face, and his bottom lip pooched out. "But sometimes you won't make me the kind of cereal I like."

"You can't have that sugary stuff *every* morning, Brady. Oh, and occasionally I grill hamburgers."

"Hamburgers?" Brady's eyes danced.

Pastor Hughes finished his iced tea, then stood up. "Who's ready to drop a line in the water?"

"Me, me, me!" Brady threw his hand up as if he were in a classroom.

"Then let's go, pardner."

≈

Jeris rinsed the last pot and placed it on the towel on the counter. "Thanks again for inviting me to dinner, Audra Darling. It was delicious as usual. But I want you to know I don't expect this all the time."

Audra Darling stood at the stovetop, wiping it with a soapy cloth. She waved the air as if dismissing Jeris's remark. "I know that. But let's approach it from this basis. If I invite you, I hope you'll accept and know I'm doing it out of genuinely wanting you to be with us and not from some sense of duty or obligation. Agreed?"

Jeris smiled at her. "Agreed. But I can never reciprocate, at least not by cooking for you. I'm sort of like Luke. I can make toast and coffee. Cereal. Bagels. Canned soup and sandwiches. But unlike him, I've never grilled—"

"You *do* need help, child." Audra Darling glanced out the window at the water as she took off her apron and smoothed the front of her pink linen suit. "Are you ready to go outside? Isn't it a glorious day?"

Jeris nodded. "The last time I was at a theme park, one of the gift shops was selling little bottles labeled *Florida Sunshine*. They looked as if they had only air in them. The clerk said they sell out so fast she can barely keep them stocked." She laughed.

Audra Darling laughed, too, then said, "I wonder if the fish are biting today, like they were yesterday. Wouldn't it be nice if that darling little Brady caught one?"

Jeris gazed out the window. "I think I can safely say he'd be as happy as if he were at Disney World. Most little boys like to catch fish." She watched Brady, Luke, and Pastor Hughes on the large square floating dock. Beyond them the sunshine danced on the pewter-colored water, a silver fish jumped in the distance, and birds flew low over the green lake grasses lining the shore. Around the rim of the water, houses were scattered here and there with docks jutting out. Across the way Jeris spotted several colorful boats—a red one, a blue one, a striped one. One boat was pulling a skier in a wide wake of water. Farther out she could see the salt marshes with their brown reedy plants.

Audra Darling bustled about the kitchen, putting away items.

Gazing at the idyllic scene through the window, Jeris was filled with a sense of peace. She couldn't wait to get out there. It was a perfect day for a water outing, not hot and not cold. It was "just right," as Goldilocks said. "It's beautiful—the water—the foliage—the boats. It's like a landscape painting come to life. It's so serene."

"That's a good way to put it. Well, I'm going to go change" —Audra Darling looked down at her suit—"into some loafing clothes. I sure couldn't take a boat ride in this, could I?" She pinched a wad of pink at her hipline.

Jeris smoothed the front of her long black skirt and over-sized matching black jacket. "These could be considered loafing clothes, I guess." She squeezed a handful of her jacket. "These jersey knits are so comfortable, even though they're professional. That's why I love to wear them. I have this suit in four different colors: black, gray, navy, and taupe." She paused. "And it doesn't take me long to get dressed every morning. That's another advantage to wearing them."

Audra Darling looked contemplative for a moment and opened her mouth as if to say something. But she turned and dashed toward the bedroom. "You go on out. I'll be there in a jiffy."

"All right." Jeris pulled open a French door. She walked out onto the porch, then down the grassy slope toward the dock. She grasped the rail and made her way onto the narrow wooden walk over the water, then to the floating dock where Pastor Hughes and Luke sat on lawn chairs.

Brady stood nearby, holding a fishing pole, his line in the water.

"Hi," she said to no one in particular, trying to be friendly. "How's it going?"

"As fine as a frog's hair and not quite as dusty." Pastor Hughes grinned as he stood. "That's what Brother Jernigan says all the time."

The three of them laughed.

Luke stood also.

"No need for you two to get up on my account." Jeris waved them back down, then walked a few steps over to Brady.

"Brother Jernigan's quite a character, isn't he?" Luke settled into his chair.

"That's an understatement." Pastor Hughes chuckled. "I'm only kidding. He's a lovable old fellow. But his antics sure keep church life exciting."

Jeris ruffled Brady's hair. Maybe it was the thickness of it. Or its unruliness—the big cowlick at the crown. It seemed everybody ruffled up his hair. "Catching any, Brady?"

He looked up at her, squinting and smiling in the sunshine, then back at the water. His pole bobbed downward. "I feel something!" he shouted. "Something's pulling my pole!"

Luke crossed the dock to Brady's side. "You've got a bite, son. You're catching a fish."

"I am?" Brady let go of his pole.

"Whoa." Luke caught it just in time and put it back in Brady's hands. "Hold on, son. You're about to bring one in."

"Yippee!"

Pastor Hughes stepped over to them.

Jeris took a step backward to give them more room. She enjoyed seeing Brady so excited.

"Bring him in, pardner." Pastor Hughes stood beside Brady, cheering him on.

Luke helped Brady pull the line out of the water, a wriggling fish on the other end.

In moments the fish was in a bucket, and Brady had already dropped his line back in the water.

"Andrew?" Audra Darling called, her voice carrying over the water as if she'd been talking into a microphone.

Jeris looked toward the house.

Audra Darling came through the French doors, leaving

them open behind her. She still had on the skirt to her pink linen suit but was wearing a yellow top.

"What's the matter, Audra?" Pastor Hughes walked briskly up the dock.

Jeris watched them as they talked. It was an emergency, from the looks of things. *Lord, help in this situation, whatever it is.*

Luke came up beside Jeris and gestured toward the house. "I hope everything's okay."

"You never know in pastoring."

He nodded somberly.

Pastor Hughes and Audra Darling walked out on the dock toward them.

"Jeris, Luke," Audra Darling said, "we need to go over to Brother Ward's house. He just died."

"I'm so sorry," Jeris said. "Is that the man you were telling me about last Sunday? The one with congestive heart failure and other complications?"

Pastor Hughes nodded. "His family called. They'd like us to come pray for them. They're pretty distraught."

"I can imagine," Jeris said. "We'll leave so you can go."

"Brady," Luke called. "We have to leave now."

"Aw, Dad." Brady's grip on his cane pole was viselike.

Audra Darling stepped forward and put her hand on Luke's forearm. "Please don't leave. Let Brady fish to his heart's content. And you and Jeris sit out here and enjoy the sunshine. And then, when Brady's finished, take a boat ride. Andrew will give you the keys. The life vests are under the seats. And then have a snack. There's plenty of sweet tea in the refrigerator and more chocolate cake on the cake plate and anything else you can find—"

"No, Audra," Luke said, "we'll go ahead and leave when you do."

"He's right," Jeris chimed in.

Pastor Hughes dug in his pocket and pulled out his key

ring. "Luke, Jeris, I insist you stay." He worked at getting a key off the ring. "Just because we have to leave doesn't mean you do. It isn't fair to disappoint Brady because we have church duties to attend to. Especially when you don't have to leave. Make yourselves at home. Take a boat ride." He placed a key in Luke's palm. "Explore some of those salt marshes I showed you the other time I took you out on the boat."

"And then go inside and get something cold to drink," Audra Darling added. "Better yet, take some cold drinks with you in the boat. There are plenty in the refrigerator, all kinds. And have some more cake before you leave."

"And when you're finished," Pastor Hughes said, "just lock up before you leave. You know where to put the spare house key."

"I—I don't know what to say," Luke said.

Jeris didn't know what to say either. The sentiments she'd felt earlier this morning when she thought Luke wanted to avoid her washed over her like a wave. And now he was hesitating to accept the Hugheses' kind offer. Probably because of her. He most likely didn't want to spend time alone with her. Well, that was fine with her. She felt the same way about him. She'd looked forward to coming to the Hugheses' house. But the original plans included Pastor Hughes and Audra Darling. Now they were leaving, and she didn't care about staying.

"We insist." Pastor Hughes and Audra Darling spoke the words at the same time.

"I know you need to go." Jeris glanced at her watch.

"And we're not leaving until you both agree to stay." Audra Darling put her hands on her hips and glared at them, a twinkle in her eyes.

Jeris glanced at Luke.

He stared at the dock and traced a knothole with the toe of his shoe. "All right. If you insist." He looked up at Pastor Hughes. "Speaking for myself, I mean. And Brady."

Jeris hesitated. Luke wouldn't look at her or give her a hint he'd like her to stay and wasn't including her in his answer. Was he just being particular in his answer? Or did he want her to leave?

"Jeris?" Audra Darling's tone was soft. "You'll stay? And you'll act as hostess in my stead? Please? I feel badly, leaving my guests."

One look at Audra Darling's pleading eyes and Jeris knew her answer. "Yes, I'll stay." She glanced over at Brady. "We'll have a good time."

five

Luke kept busy with Brady for nearly an hour, not necessarily avoiding Jeris, who was sitting quietly behind them on a lawn chair, but because Brady needed his help. He had caught two fish. And then four times fish had nabbed his bait, which meant the hook had to be baited over and over.

He'd already cleaned Brady's fish, scales flying everywhere. That way the chore would be done when they were ready to go. He didn't intend to stick around long.

He saw several fish scales on his sleeve and flicked them off. Another reason he hadn't talked to Jeris was because she hadn't talked to him. She was a reticent one.

He swiped at his sweaty forehead with his arm. His hands were too nasty with fish smell to use right now. On the weathered dock, with the sun beating down and not a breeze to stir the air, it felt almost as hot as summertime. But the sun felt good. He liked the outdoors and the activities associated with it: trail biking, swimming, jogging, hiking—just about anything under the brilliant blue sky.

One more swipe at his forehead and he wondered how Jeris was standing the heat in her black jacket and long skirt.

He glanced over at the boat. Before they left to go home they needed to take a boat ride, what the Hugheses had insisted they do. "Brady, are you ready for a boat ride?"

"Yippee!" Brady threw his pole on the dock and raced toward the boat.

"Whoa, Little Man. Don't get too close to the edge. Get back now."

Brady stepped back.

"That's good."

"Can we go now? Can we go now?" Brady was doing his usual jumping.

"In a minute." Luke cleaned his hands with disposable wet cloths from Pastor Hughes's tackle box, then helped Brady do the same. He noticed Jeris still hadn't said a word. What was going on with her? Hadn't she heard them talking about the boat ride? "Jeris, are you ready to take a boat ride? We won't stay out very long." Still cleaning his hands, he turned around to face her.

"I guess so." She had taken off her black jacket and wore a brown sleeveless shirt. She fanned her hand in front of her neck, her olive skin looking tanner than usual—no doubt the result of the sunshine today. She stood up and stretched. "But why don't I do what Audra Darling suggested and get some soft drinks for us to have in the boat?"

"I'll vote for that." Luke closed the tackle box. "I'm as thirsty as a straggler in the Sahara."

"Miss Jeris, can you bring me a root beer?" Brady asked.

"I sure will. If Audra Darling has any."

"Anything is fine for me."

"Okay. I'll be right back." She turned and headed up to the house.

Ten minutes later they were seated in the boat, life vests on and drinking their cold beverages, not saying anything, just enjoying the drinks in the warm sunshine.

Jeris reached into a plastic grocery bag she'd brought along and retrieved three baseball caps. She handed two of them to Luke and Brady.

"Where did you get these?" Luke asked.

"Inside. On a rack. I figured Pastor Hughes wouldn't mind our borrowing them. He has at least two dozen, and they'll be a lifesaver out here in the sun."

"Thanks." Luke put on his hat, and Brady did, too.

She set her soft drink down on the bottom of the boat and balanced it between her shoes. She removed an elastic band from her wrist, shook out her hair, gathered it into a ponytail, and secured it with the band. Then she put on the cap and carefully threaded her ponytail through the hole in the back.

Luke couldn't help watching her. She wasn't three feet away from him in the boat. For some reason her movements bothered him. They were almost. . .intimate?

She adjusted the bill of her cap.

He noticed she'd taken off her black tights when she went inside. Good. At least she wouldn't be so hot. But she still had on her ugly black shoes. *Sturdy* was how he'd describe them, not like Audra's, those sandal-like heels many women wore.

"This tastes good, Miss Jeris." Brady held up his root beer and smiled his charming smile at her.

"This does, too, Brady." She held up her drink and smiled back. "I think Audra Darling would say you're a darling boy."

Brady giggled, his shoulders shaking, his nose scrunched up.

"Everybody about finished?" Luke had his hand on the key. "Ready to go?"

"In a minute, Dad." Brady held his drink to his lips and drained the bottle.

"One more sip and I'll be ready, too." Jeris collected their bottles and put them in the grocery bag, then put the bag in a side compartment. "Okay."

"Me, too, Dad. Let's go."

"Hang on," Luke yelled, "as we go sailing into the wide, blue yonder!"

"Only we don't have a sail," she added wryly.

Luke smiled.

She held on to the rail beside the seat and told Brady to do the same. Then she reached for his other hand and kept it in hers.

They took off across the river, the wind in their faces. Luke enjoyed the cooling breeze. For close to half an hour he drove, weaving into small fingers of water that extended into the salt marshes, then out again into broad expanses. Pastor

Hughes had recently studied salt marshes, and Luke recalled some terms he had used. *Salinity*. Spartina, *a type of cord-grass abundant in the marsh. Spot-tail bass. Blue crab. Shrimp. Alligators, though rare.*

Luke reduced the speed so he could be heard. He wanted to tell Brady something Pastor Hughes had told him. "Brady, Pastor Hughes says you can sometimes see a manatee out here. So be on the lookout."

"Oh, boy! Like the ones we saw on TV last year?"

Luke smiled. It was last week. "Yes, just like those. Manatees are marine mammals, remember? And remember how the documentary called manatees 'gentle giants'? And it said some people call them 'sea cows.'"

"I want to see a sea cow." Brady grasped the side of the boat and leaned over.

"Be careful, Brady." Jeris had let go of his hand at the lower speed but reached for him now and grabbed a handful of his shirt for safety.

"What do manatees eat, Dad?"

"They're herbivores."

"What's that mean?"

"It means they eat plants." Jeris kept her grasp firm on Brady's shirt.

"Oh."

"They feed on water grasses, hyacinths, mangrove leaves, things like that," Jeris said. "I've seen them all my life. I grew up in Florida."

"Me, too," Brady said.

"The documentary said they consume up to 9 percent of their body weight every day." Luke searched the water close to the boat and farther away near the reedlike grasses. He hoped they'd see a manatee for Brady's sake.

"I want a snack, Dad."

"How about a water lily?" Luke laughed.

"Da–a–a–d."

"I'm only kidding. When we get back we'll have another piece of Audra's chocolate cake. How about that? She said to help ourselves."

"Yippee!"

Luke turned off the motor and let the boat float. "Maybe the quiet will bring a manatee to us."

Jeris nodded.

"So you grew up in Florida?" Luke kept his voice low. "In Winter Haven, right? Isn't that what Pastor Hughes said, the Sunday you told us about the children's church program?"

"Yes. In Winter Haven. Where are you from?"

"I'm a native Floridian, too, but I'm not from around here. I grew up in Ocala."

"Pretty area. Horse farms and rolling hills."

He nodded.

"I have an aunt who lives not far from Ocala. When I was growing up, we used to visit her. But I haven't been up that way in ages. How long have you lived in Silver Bay?"

"A little over four years," he said.

"Dad!" Brady shouted. "I have to go to the bathroom!"

"Brady. There's such a thing as manners." He looked straight ahead, not even glancing at Jeris.

Brady jumped up, sending the boat rocking.

"Sit down, Little Man. You'll turn us over."

Brady sat back down. "But I've got to go bad, Dad."

Jeris was laughing.

Luke felt embarrassed. "Brady, you'll have to wait," he said in a low, controlled voice.

"I can't." Brady's feet were dancing on the bottom of the boat, making *tap*, *tap*, *tap* noises.

Jeris put her arm around Brady and smiled at him. "We can't predict when nature calls, can we, Little Man? I guess your great big root beer took a great big toll." She glanced over at Luke and shrugged. "Can you find a place for him to get out?"

Brady's upper body was now shaking.

"Looks like you'll have to," she added.

Luke nodded, cranked the motor, and headed for the closest shore. When he stopped, Brady jumped into the shallow water and headed for land. "Brady, I was going to get out and pull the boat up so you wouldn't get wet."

"I can't wait, Dad."

Luke jumped into the water, sneakers and jeans and all. He needed to guide Brady, his mind on crabs—and alligators. He shuddered as he caught up to him and grabbed his hand. "Come on, Little Man." They took off through the shallow water. "Jeris, can you throw the anchor over the side? We'll be right back."

"I'll 'sit tight,' as Audra Darling says. And I'll take care of the anchor for you."

"Thanks." Luke looked for a sheltered place some distance from Jeris and headed that way with his son.

"Dad, can we go exploring?" Brady asked when they came out from the shelter of trees.

Luke glanced around and saw a copse of trees. Leading into it were some rough trails that probably hadn't been walked on in a long time. "I don't know. . . ."

"Please, Dad? We can pretend we're Christopher Columbus."

Luke smiled. Brady's first-grade class had studied Columbus last week. "Jeris is with us. She probably wouldn't like to go traipsing about in the woods."

"Miss Jeris!" Brady turned toward her and flailed his arms in the air like a windmill. "Can you come over here?"

Luke looked across the way at the boat.

Jeris leaned forward and cupped her ear as if she were trying to hear what Brady was saying.

"Brady, if she's going with us, we need to be gentlemen and help her out of the boat."

"Okay, Dad."

Luke grabbed Brady's hand, and they dashed toward the

edge of the water then stopped.

"What did you say, Brady?"

"I'm going to be Christopher Columbus, Miss Jeris."

Luke smiled. "Brady wants to follow a trail into the woods. I know it's getting late. But we won't be long, that is, if it's all right with you. Do you want to go? If you don't, we won't do it. We wouldn't want to impose."

"Please, Miss Jeris?" Brady folded his hands in his familiar prayer stance, jumping on one foot, then the other.

She laughed. "I—" She glanced down at her clothing.

"You're not dressed for hiking. . . ." Luke's voice trailed off. *That long skirt. . . .* "Can you walk in the woods in that thing?"

"Hey, I'll manage. I'm tough. I accept the invitation."

"Yippee!"

"I love traipsing through the woods," she said.

"Okay. But don't climb out yet, okay?"

"Okay."

"I'll pull the boat up on the bank so you won't get wet." Luke turned to Brady. "Stay put." He sloshed through the water to the back of the boat, threw the anchor inside, and pushed the boat with a hard thrust. Then he came around to the front, pulled it onto dry ground, and held out his hand to her.

Jeris stood up, took his hand, and stepped toward him, rocking the boat. She stopped. "Yikes."

Luke clamped down on the side of the boat and steadied it.

"Thanks."

"Try again."

She took another step, then started to climb over the side. *R–r–i–i–i–p.*

"My skirt." She looked down. The side slit was now several inches higher, and the fabric was jagged where it tore.

"Oh, my." Luke looked at Brady. "We didn't mean to tear her clothes, did we, Brady?" He felt bad that her skirt was ruined.

Brady's giggles filled the air.

"No problem. Maybe it can be fixed. If not, I'll buy a new

one." Her hand still firmly in his, she jumped over the side and landed solidly on two feet.

Good thing she's wearing those—those—oxfords?

She smiled at Luke, then ran her hand through Brady's hair. "Who's ready for an adventure? I am."

"Yippee!" Brady shouted.

"Let's go, Christopher Columbus."

❧

Luke sat down by Brady in his twin bed that night and pulled the sheet up to his chest. He handed him a book from the bedside table, then picked up another book and thumbed through it.

"We had the goodest time today, didn't we, Dad?"

Luke smiled. Brady said that every time he had a good time. "You need to say *best* not *goodest*."

Brady looked up at him with a puzzled expression on his face.

"Oh, never mind." Luke affectionately tapped Brady's chin. He was too young to grasp grammar. There would be plenty of time for that later. My, how he loved this child. Little Man—what he'd dubbed him the first time he laid eyes on him.

He felt. . .how did he feel? He looked down at the book he was holding and saw the word *fuzzy* in the story. That's how he felt. Pleasant images filled his mind. Brady in his school uniform coming out of the front door of his school. Where had the time gone? How could he be in school already? Brady in swimming trunks, jumping into their pool. They'd had some good times together in the backyard. He was glad he'd decided to put in a pool. Brady dressed up in his Sunday clothes, holding his children's Bible and full of questions about Moses and other Bible characters. Brady with his ear-to-ear smile and little freckled face and unruly blond hair. He added joy to Luke's life.

Brady picked up another book from the bedside table and opened it.

Luke thought about the busy week ahead. He would be out three nights. A dinner, a club meeting, and another function he couldn't remember. That meant he wouldn't be there to put him to bed and read to him those nights as he was about to do now. And Wednesday nights were out, too, for bedtime reading. They were always a scramble—church, a quick bath, a prayer, and a kiss. That left just three nights for their ritual.

If only there were more days in the week. Good thing he wasn't dating.

"Look, Dad." Brady held his book so Luke could see the page. "This little boy's fishing, just like I did today. I caught two fishes. All by myself."

Luke looked at the picture. A little boy was pulling on a fishing pole. On the end of the line was a fish. "You sure did, Brady." He caressed Brady's sun-reddened cheeks. "I was proud of you." He tweaked him on the nose. "You're growing up too fast."

Brady pushed up his pajama sleeve and flexed his muscle. "I'm big, Dad, aren't I?"

"Yes, you are."

"Feel it." He thrust his arm out and flexed his muscle again.

Luke squeezed Brady's arm. "It's as hard as a rock."

Brady had that little-boy proud look. "It took some big muscles to catch those fishes today, didn't it, Dad?"

"It sure did. Which did you like best? Fishing? The boat ride? Or our walk in the woods?"

"The goodest part was when Miss Jeris was climbing out of the boat and her skirt went *r–r–i–i–i–p*." A fit of giggles hit him, and the bed shook with his laughter. "That was so funny."

Luke distinctly remembered the moment.

"She's fun, isn't she, Dad?"

Luke tickled him along the ribs, and Brady shrieked like a fire truck.

He buried the top of his head in Brady's chest, then gave him a bear hug. "You're funner, Little Man."

six

Luke stuck his head in the church library and saw the volunteer librarian—a rotund elderly lady—sitting at a desk, engrossed in a book and munching on a cookie. "Miss Ada?"

She threw her hand over her generous bosom. "Mercy me, you scared the wits out of me." Her chest heaved in and out, and the little veins on her nose turned as red as a candied apple. She fanned herself with her lace-trimmed handkerchief.

He walked to the desk and smiled at her. "I'm sorry, Miss Ada. I didn't mean to startle you."

"I guess I was so enthralled with my book—" She stopped talking, fidgeted, and put her hand over the book she'd been reading.

Luke couldn't help seeing the cover. It depicted a man and a woman in a tasteful embrace. Since the library was in the church, he was sure it was a wholesome Christian novel. He squelched a smile—not at the book but at the way she was trying to hide it. Miss Ada was at least seventy. She was the proverbial old maid of the congregation.

"I didn't even hear the door open. Normally it creaks."

He laughed. Most doors in this church creaked.

"I have a title to recommend to you before you leave." She adjusted her glasses. "But, first, did you need to tell me something? You're a man on a mission, aren't you? I can tell by the look on your face. You're definitely not one of my regular patrons. You do much reading? Do you ever read those new Christian novels they're publishing nowadays? I do. Of course I don't get them from this library."

She rolled her eyes. "We haven't had a new book in Christ Church library for more than fifteen years. I check out Christian novels from the public library." She reeled off a few authors' names. "Have you read any of their new books?"

"I. . .can't say that I have. I'm not into fiction."

"Well, you should be. Promise me you'll try them. I know you'd like them. Okay?"

"Okay, Miss Ada. I will."

"But you didn't come here to check out a book, did you? Or hear about new titles, right?"

"Right." He cleared his throat. "Pastor Hughes assigned me to the church library, and I was stopping by to check—"

"Hmmph!" She turned up her nose. "Why don't you deacons fix the creaking doors around here and quit snooping in places you have no business in?"

He didn't say anything at first. The last deacon overseeing the library ministry hadn't been able to accomplish anything, with Miss Ada being so snippy and all. That deacon had finally given up. That was three years ago, Pastor Hughes had told him.

He took a step toward her and smiled his most engaging smile. "Miss Ada, I stopped by to tell you I have a five-hundred-dollar donation for you to buy some new books."

She jumped up, bustled around the desk, and pulled him toward her in a big hug. "Well, I'll say." She hugged him again.

Luke caught a whiff of dusting powder, the scent his grandmother used. Something purple-sounding. Lavender? Lilac?

"Happy hoedown and all that stuff." She danced a little reel, her elbows flailing chicken-style. "Where did that kind of donation come from?"

"Sorry. I can't tell. It's anonymous. But the donor requested that half of it be spent on children's books."

"Children's?" She stopped in her tracks, her sparse gray eyebrows pulled down over her thick glasses. "I haven't had a child in this library in the twenty-two years I've been working here."

"Maybe because you don't have any children's books."

"Well, I can remedy that now, can't I? I'll be glad to pick out some. That'll be nice, spending other people's money. But stuff and nonsense—I want to assure you it's not my fault we haven't had any children's books in here—except for a few."

"No, I wouldn't blame you at all, Miss Ada."

She thrust her hand out sideways, indicating a shelf with only three or four thin children's books. "I've been a public-school librarian and know what a library needs to make it good. Variety—and that includes children's books. I know that as well as I know my name. But I never had funds to buy them. And whenever I asked for book donations, I only received ones for adults. And you'd be surprised at what some of those were."

She leaned forward, her eyes widening, and lowered her voice. "Racy romances, that's what." She wagged her finger at him. "Anonymous, of course. Just like this donated money you told me about."

She tsk-tsked. "Yessirreebob, one Sunday morning when I arrived, a pasteboard box was sitting by the door. When I went through it I found some of those. . .those. . .well, the kind of books I just told you about. There's no place in a church library for books like that."

"Only books like this." Luke whisked the book she'd been reading from her desk and held it up. He couldn't resist. He smiled again.

"Right as rain." She took the book from him and brandished it in the air like a politician making a point. "This"—she thumped the cover—"is a good book. It entertains you, and it draws you to God in the process."

He patted her shoulder. "I'm only teasing you, Miss Ada."

She shrugged away. "Well, I'm *not* teasing. I'm speaking a truth here," she said in an authoritative tone.

"I'm sure you are, though I can't attest to the glowing review of the book you're reading." He glanced at the cover. "As I said, I don't read much fiction. And I've never read in that genre."

"Maybe you should." Merriment danced in her faded blue eyes. She held up the book and tapped on the picture of the couple. "Boy meets girl. Boy resists girl. True love wins out. Boy gets girl. And they live happily ever after."

He laughed. Then he glanced at his watch. "Well, I need to pick up Brady from his class."

"How's that boy doing in school? He's a charmer if ever I saw one."

"He's doing fine, Miss Ada. He loves it. He can't wait to get there every morning."

"Every time he sees me, he gives me a great big hug. Makes a person feel as dear as the apple of one's eye. And he's so polite."

"Thank you. He's my Little Man." The warm fuzziness he often felt when he was with Brady hit him now.

"It was you, wasn't it?" She peered into his eyes. "The donor?"

"No. But I wish I'd thought of it first." He glanced around at the meager selection of books. He'd never been in the church library. "It's an excellent idea."

She put her hand on his arm. "I'm grateful for it. Honest I am. Please express my thanks to Pastor Hughes. And if you know who donated the money, please tell them I said thank you. And"—she paused and drew a lungful of air—"I apologize for being so. . .so. . .bristly when you first came in."

He patted her shoulder. "That's okay, Miss Ada."

She walked over to her desk and picked up a pamphletlike book. "I've been doing some work in here, contrary to what you deacons think." She winked at him. "I'm not meaning that in a harsh way, honest." She winked again. "And when I was sorting through the shelves I came across an interesting book I'd like to recommend to you."

He looked down at the faded booklet in her hands and scanned the title. *"How to Choose the Right Wife. . .for Christian Lads."*

"Luke, I think it would be good for you to read it."

He bit his bottom lip. *Oh, no, here it comes.* Advice about his *situation*. But then he smiled, somewhat interested in what this colorful lady had to say.

"You know. Your situation and all."

He felt like playfully rolling his eyes. But he kept his gaze steady instead. "Yes?"

"Frankly, I'm not one to be pushy."

He squelched a grin.

"But when I pulled this book off the shelf it piqued my interest, and I sat down then and there and read it from cover to cover." She held the thin book gingerly, as if it might fall apart from age. "Actually, when I saw it, the first person I thought of was you."

"Me?"

"Yessirreebob. It was the Sunday your Brady made his prayer request during morning worship."

"Oh." Luke rocked on his heels, remembering his embarrassment with a sharp poignancy.

"Soon as I read it, I asked the Lord to bring you into my library so I could give it to you."

"You did?"

"I did. And He did."

"Right as rain?" He laughed as he used her expression.

She laughed with him.

"Technically, though, wasn't it Pastor Hughes who sent me in here?"

She shook her head, the soft part of her full jowls jiggling. "Nosirreebob. It was God. I know it because I asked Him to, and the Bible says, 'Ask, and it shall be given you.' I prayed, and He answered."

He looked down at the title again.

"Even though it was written in 1954, its truths still apply today."

"In 1954?" He nodded slowly, gazing at the cover. What

did a book that old have to say, especially about *that* subject? He envisioned women dressed like those in *Little House on the Prairie*, even though he knew that era was the 1800s. But the images wouldn't leave. He chuckled.

"Don't you go laughing till you see what's in it." She looked at him, a twinkle in her eyes. She opened the booklet, moved closer to him so he could see the pages, and ran her finger down the table of contents. " 'Make Sure God Is Involved,' " she read. "That's the first chapter. Here's the second: 'What Kind of Girl to Look For.' And another: 'How Can You Tell If It's the Real McCoy?' " She closed the booklet and held it out. "It has some good things to say about choosing a wife."

To be polite, Luke took the booklet from her. "Thank you, Miss Ada."

She grasped his hand and squeezed it. "You promise me you'll read it?"

He was as interested in reading it as he was in reading *The Iliad*. "I—" He noted its thinness. It would take him maybe thirty minutes. Or less. "Sure."

"Then come over here and check it out." She sat down at her desk and thumbed through a small wooden box, then glanced up at him. "I know my system's archaic. But we have so few books."

"Soon you'll have some new ones. And maybe more donations will start coming in."

"I hope so." She bent over the small box again. "Let's see." Her eyebrows drew together as she kept thumbing. "Here it is." She pulled out a yellowed index card, wrote his name and the date on it, then handed the booklet to him.

"Thanks."

"You can keep it as long as you want. It hasn't been checked out since 1955."

seven

Jeris finished her client dictation, then tidied her desk. She couldn't get her mind off ten-year-old Lane Felton. His mother, a single mom, had dropped dead three weeks ago at the age of thirty-seven, apparently from a heart attack. His grandmother was bringing him twice a week so Jeris could help him deal with his shock and grief.

"Lord," she prayed, clasping her hands on top of her desk, "please help Lane. Holy Spirit, bring Your comfort into his little heart. Surround him like a cocoon and gather him into Your tender, loving arms. Assure him that You love him and that he'll make it through this trying time—"

Z-z-z-z-z. It was her cell phone vibrating. Z-z-z-z-z.

She picked it up, saw Audra Darling's number on the display, and clicked it on. "Hi, Audra Darling."

"Hi, Jeris. Are you on your way home?"

"No, I'm still at the office."

"You sound like Luke. Work, work, work. That's all you two know how to do." Audra Darling's laughter rippled through the phone lines.

"I'm on my way out. I had a heavy case load today, and I just finished the last of my notes."

"I'll catch you later then."

"No, that's okay." Jeris stood and slung her purse over her shoulder. "I can talk." She picked up her briefcase. "Now is as good a time as any," she said, walking toward the door.

"You sure?"

Jeris stepped outside the building and locked the glass door. "I'm sure."

"You told me to call you."

"I did?" She reached her car.

Audra Darling laughed. "Sounds like you need a glass of sweet iced tea to wind down."

"Or a fat-free latte." Jeris got into her SUV and started the engine.

"I'm calling about the party we need to plan for children's church."

"Oh." Jeris pulled out of the parking lot and threaded into traffic on the busy road. "I haven't thought about it since—"

"Let me guess. Since last Sunday when we talked. That's when you told me to call you."

"Right. I remember now."

"You said something about taking the kids on a picnic?"

"Don't you think they'd like that? Somewhere away from the church? Something different? And fun?"

"Yes, they'd love it. I was reading an article in the newspaper this morning about a beach not far from here where you can hunt for sharks' teeth."

"Sharks' teeth?"

"Prehistoric sharks' teeth, according to the article."

Jeris's mind went into overdrive. *We can have a picnic on the beach and then hunt for sharks' teeth.* She made a left-hand turn, and the phone fell from its perch on her shoulder. *And then I can teach them a brief lesson about Jonah and the whale.* She put the phone back up to her ear. *Only I'll tell the kids the Bible says it was a great fish, not necessarily a whale, and that some Bible scholars say it could've been a large shark and—*

"Jeris? Did you hear me?"

"I sort of did. My phone fell, and by the time I picked it up, well, what you said was spotty."

"I said we could take them. . ." Audra Darling proceeded to give voice to everything Jeris had been thinking.

Jeris laughed. "Sounds fabulous. When I dropped the phone I was mapping out the party exactly as you did, down to the lesson on Jonah and the whale."

"When the Holy Spirit illuminates minds, you never know what's going to happen." Audra Darling laughed. "If it's all right with you, I'll plan the party for you. The food, the transportation, things like that. In fact I've already done a few things. I figured it would help you out—"

"It'd be a big help."

"I'll get a chaperone. Counting us, that'll be three. Don't you think that's how many we should have? Considering the kids'll be on the beach and we'll need to keep a close eye on them?"

"Sounds like a good plan. Who are you planning to call?" *Not Luke Moore, I hope.* At the Hugheses' parsonage Luke had been polite to her, but that was about all she could say for him. Oh, yes. She could add *cold* and *aloof.*

"I thought I'd call Luke."

Not him. "What about Denny Roper's grandmother? She's the one who brings him to church. She always shows an interest in things that concern him. She might go with us."

"She's tied up."

"Why not Cheryl Carson? She brings her neighbor's son, Jeffrey, and she might be willing."

"I tried her, too."

"What about Blake Larsen's mother or father?"

"They're going out of town on a business trip, and his grandmother's keeping him. I asked her, but she has two other grandchildren she's watching that day, and they're babies. I can't think of anyone else."

"Looks as if it'll be Luke then?"

"If he agrees."

"I've got the joy, joy, joy, joy down in my heart," she sang inside. Only the children's song was dirgelike. She didn't want Luke to think she was behind this. She didn't want him thinking she was on his trail. Because she wasn't. He clearly wasn't interested in her. And she clearly wasn't interested in him. And never would be.

eight

After Luke put Brady to bed, he set his iced tea glass on the lamp table in the family room, stretched out on the sofa, and picked up the remote, working the throw pillow behind his head to get it just right. He aimed the remote, turned on the TV, and flipped channels. He flipped through them again. He punched in numbers. He punched in other numbers. He flipped all the way through the channels for the third time, from the lowest to the highest.

I have an evening designated for downtime and no work, and wouldn't you know? I can't find a thing to watch. He clicked off the TV.

Maybe he would catch a short snooze. It was too early to go to bed. Only 8:45. He glanced at the dark TV. Well, he could always work. He looked across the room into the kitchen and saw his briefcase sitting by the door. He'd brought home extra work in case he found some free time.

All right then, he would get some work done. He stretched both arms, his hand hitting the lamp behind him. He sprang up, swung around, and caught the lamp just in time. He set it upright and adjusted the shade. On the lamp table was his Bible. Sticking out from the middle of the Bible was the little book Miss Ada had given him last Sunday.

How to Choose the Right Wife. . .for Christian Lads.

He'd promised her he'd read it. Now would be a good time. He picked it up. "Let's see, Mr."—he noticed the author's name on the cover—"Granfield, if you can tell this lad how to choose a wife." He smiled as he turned to chapter one: "Make .Sure God Is Involved."

"The Creator of the heavens and the earth, the Eternal One who is omniscient, omnipresent, and omnipotent, created you, His masterpiece and highest work of creation. Though He manages the vast universe, He wants to be involved in your life, and most particularly whom you marry."

I'll agree with that. Luke took a sip of iced tea.

"God's Word is your road map on the Seeking Road as you make your way toward Marriage City."

Interesting way to put it.

"As you serve God and put Him first in your life, He will lead you in the path He's chosen for you. Your duty is to ask Him to show you His will and way. Let me assure you this will not be a bitter pill to swallow. Conversely, it will bring you joy, for God is a God of infinite joy. Walking in His will, you will be the happiest.

The girl God has for you will be tailor-made for you. Even if she doesn't have rose-petal lips, cute dimples, and curly hair, you will think she's the darlingest thing on earth."

Luke laughed so hard that he nearly dropped his glass. This sounded as if Audra had written it.

"Some lads pray about their spiritual lives. That's commendable. Some even pray about such things as their jobs, all the way down to the mundane. That, too, is admirable. But God wants you to pray about choosing a mate, the right person, the wife He has planned for you. His Word says in Jeremiah 29:11 that He has definite plans for you. He wants you to seek Him in earnest prayer about one of the most important plans in your life—The Marriage Plan. Have you done that? If not, I advise you to stop reading right now and commit your way to Him, as the scripture says."

Luke laid the booklet aside and put his glass on the lamp table. He'd prayed about many things: the church, its ministries, Pastor Hughes and Audra. He'd prayed about career moves, the right school for Brady, even whether or not to put a pool in his backyard last summer. But he had never prayed about The Marriage Plan.

I've never asked God to send me a mate. And not just any mate, but His choice for my life.

He snapped his eyes shut. "Lord, I'm sorry I haven't prayed about this before. I took this part of my life for granted. I thought it would just happen in its own time. But now I want to commit my way to You, as this little book teaches. From now on I'm relying on You to bring a woman into my life, the right woman who's tailor-made for me."

He drew a deep breath. "Please prepare my heart. Whatever needs changing in me, please do it. I'm open and willing. In Jesus' name. Amen."

❧

Luke dove into the swimming pool, then surfaced, swam to the side, and called for Brady to get in the deep end with him.

Brady jumped in, went under, and came up, his little arms flailing in the water.

Luke grabbed hold of him, and Brady clung to his neck. "Want to swim across the pool, Little Man?"

Brady nodded and started out.

"Go, Brady! You can do it." Luke dog-paddled nearby as Brady swam across the pool. He was staying close for safety. "Go, go, go. Keep those arms digging into that water. Keep those feet kicking. That's it. Go, boy! Go!"

Brady surfaced at the other side and hung on to the tiled

lower edge, swilling in big gulps of air, his chest going up and down, his face all smiles. "I did it, Dad. I did it."

"Yes, you did. Congratulations."

"Am I a good swimmer, Dad?"

"The best."

Brady pulled himself along the side of the pool as he made his way to the shallow end. "I'm going to get my mask and fins."

"Okay, Little Man. But don't let go of the edge. You're still in the deep end."

"I won't, Dad."

Luke leaned back against the side, his elbows resting on the tiled lower edge. He was glad for this time with Brady. He'd left work early today and picked him up at the afternoon care center.

He looked at the sky. They had at least another hour of daylight. Each spring day that edged toward summer gave them longer daylight hours, and he was taking advantage of it every chance he could. Tomorrow night he and Brady were going to a PTA meeting, and Wednesday night was church. Thursday night he would be at a board meeting, and Friday night he had to go to a banquet. His week would be gone in a blink of the eye.

Saturday Brady was attending the children's church picnic out on the beach. That was perfect. Luke was going on a boating outing with some of his clients. A group of people aboard six or seven boats would spend the day together, picnicking, swimming, and skiing. One of the clients had just bought a cabin cruiser, and he'd told Luke he couldn't wait to try it out. Luke couldn't either. "We'll have a high old time," the client had said.

With Brady taken care of, Luke could attend the outing and not feel guilty about leaving him. His son would be having his own high old time.

"Look, Dad. I'm going to stand on my hands under the water."

Luke glanced at the decorative clock on the wall of the lanai. He needed to get the hamburgers on the grill.

"Da–a–a–d, look."

"I'm looking." He pinned his gaze on Brady. It was funny how kids wanted their parents to look at them all the time. But it was also satisfying for parents to do so. To kids it meant their parents were pretty much the center of their little worlds. He liked being the center of Brady's world.

Brady went down headfirst into the water and stuck his legs up, his little fins waving like flags in the air. Then he burst up to the surface. "Did you see me, Dad? Did you see me?"

"I sure did. Good going. You held your breath a long time. And you balanced perfectly."

R–r–r–i–i–ing.

Luke bounded out of the water, walked over to the table near the shallow end, and, still keeping his eyes on Brady, grabbed the phone. He scanned the display and clicked it on. "Hi, Audra."

"Hi, Luke. Busy?"

"I'm about to throw some hamburgers on the grill. Brady and I are outside swimming."

"The life of Riley."

"I wish."

"Just kidding. That's the biggest tale of all, accusing you of being lazy. I'm calling because we need a chaperone for the children's church picnic on Saturday—"

"I'm tied up."

"You are?"

He could hear disappointment in her voice. "I have an outing with some clients."

"Oh."

Several seconds passed.

"Audra? Did we get cut off?"

"No."

"I'm sorry I can't help."

"It's okay. I understand. Work's work."

A high old time.

"Well, I won't keep you from the pool and Brady. I'm sure we'll manage."

He felt bad about disappointing her. But he couldn't help it that he had plans. Surely she could find someone else.

They said good-bye, and he clicked off the phone.

"Who was that, Dad?" Brady was standing on the top step of the shallow end, throwing colorful diving toys into the bottom of the pool.

"Audra Hughes. She was talking about the children's church party."

"I can't wait till Saturday, Dad."

"You mean because of the party?"

"No. I get to see Miss Jeris again."

༄

Luke left Brady's bedroom and settled onto the sofa. It was time for session number two with *How to Choose the Right Wife. . .for Christian Lads*. What would Mr. Granfield tell him tonight?

He opened the booklet to chapter two: "What Kind of Girl to Look For."

"Never look down on yourself because you are searching for a mate. Just as a garden needs rain, so a lad needs a wife. It's the same way for a girl, too. She needs a husband. But the question is, what kind of a mate do you look for?

God has created lads and girls with certain physical attributes. Lads like girls with feminine charm, much like the old nursery rhyme says, 'Sugar and spice and everything nice.' Girls like lads with masculine traits, such as broad shoulders and strong muscles. God planned these things when He created Adam and Eve. He also planned that there would be basic physical needs in both lads and girls. But they are to be fulfilled only within the bonds of holy matrimony. Marriage will be the culmination of your God-created physical longings.

While marriage is an honorable institution that should

be sought, you are not to go into it unadvisedly. Lad, you
are not to be swayed by a girl with curls."

Oh, brother.

"If God thought enough of your brain to wrap a skull
around it, He expects you to use it."

That's a profound statement, Luke thought. *I need to memorize
that. It'll help me at work. And in teaching Brady when he reaches
his teenage years.*

"The field to choose a mate from is narrow for the
Christian lad. There are restrictions, but they are for
your own good. The girl you choose must be a genuine
Christian. The Bible boldly proclaims this when it says
you must not be unequally yoked. Do not permit yourself
to look outside the ranks of the righteous."

I'm on the right track there.

"Don't rush into a relationship. Take your time. Do not
have a whirlwind courtship."

I'm good to go. I'm in full agreement.

"It's very important to get the right girl. You will not
only have a physical union with your mate but a spiritual
one. Two souls shall be one. You will share laughter and
tears, joy and heartache, life and death.

Think on the girls you know. This is where you must
start looking. There is a tender love story in the Old
Testament about Ruth and Boaz. When Ruth and
Naomi came to Judah, the hand of God guided Ruth
into the field of Boaz. He was someone with whom she

and Naomi were familiar. Likewise, he knew of Ruth. Her sweetness and industriousness impressed him, and he eventually wooed and won her hand in marriage.

Again, I tell you, think on the girls you know."

Think on the girls I know? The only single ones he knew at church were Miss Ada and Jeris Waldron.

"Do not necessarily look for sweeping eyelashes and wavy hair. The pretty ones with the pink cheeks and hourglass figures might not have those pink cheeks and hourglass figures after marriage."

Luke laughed out loud.

"A girl with average looks oftentimes supersedes a glamour queen. A glamour queen, while she may catch your eye before marriage, might also catch other lads' eyes—after marriage to you. Just because a girl has blue eyes and raven hair and peaches-and-cream skin means nothing in the lifetime you will share together. Sometimes the beautiful-on-the-outside girl expects you to wait on her hand and foot. She might be conceited and selfish.

Do not think I am putting down beauty. I am just warning you. A word to the wise is sufficient, the Bible says.

However, lad, it is important to note here that you are not required to marry a girl as ugly as a weathered barn, no matter how good a Christian she is. You are not required to marry a butterface girl. What is that, you ask? A man got married, and his coworker asked him what his wife looked like. 'She's a butterface girl.' 'A butterface girl?' the coworker asked. 'Yes, she's pretty everywhere but her face.'"

Luke closed the booklet. He was laughing too hard to continue.

nine

On the Friday night before the children's beach party, Luke dialed Audra's number.

"Hi, Luke. 'Sup? as the kids say."

"What does that mean?"

"What's up?"

Luke chuckled. "Oh."

"Working with children will keep you up on the latest jargon—and keep you young."

"You're saying I'm going to pull a fast one on Father Time tomorrow?"

"You're going to chaperone the children's beach party?"

"If you still need me."

"Do we ever. Luke, that's great. We appreciate it."

"Glad I can help. Do I need to arrive early?"

"Just come at the time I told you to bring Brady. Eight o'clock will be fine." She filled him in on the details: what their plans were and what they needed him to do before, during, and after the outing.

"I'll see you then, Audra."

"Wait, Luke. May I ask you a question?"

"Shoot."

"How come you're available? What happened?"

"My plans fell through." He didn't tell her his client's brand-new cabin cruiser hadn't been ready on time, and the client had to cancel the boating party for tomorrow.

"I'm sorry to hear that. But I'm glad you're coming with us. Brady'll love having his dad along for the outing. I think it'll mean something to him."

"I'm looking forward to being with him, too, at his class

party. Wouldn't Jeris's term for that be *bonding*?"

"I think so."

"Whatever it's called, Brady is worth all my time."

"Luke?"

"What?"

"I prayed this would happen."

"That what would happen?"

"That you'd go with us."

"You did?"

"Well, my actual prayer was, 'Lord, I'd really like Luke to go with us on Saturday, but let Your will be done.' It appears it's His will for you to go, wouldn't you say? But time will tell."

He didn't know what to say. "Well," he finally managed, "I'll see you tomorrow morning, Audra."

"Okay, Luke. Thanks again."

He clicked off the phone and hurriedly made his way into the family room. Miss Ada's booklet was beckoning.

❧

Luke picked up the book and made himself comfortable on the sofa. He turned to the next chapter, "Inward Beauty Is the Most Important Kind."

"Lad, search for a beautiful woman, meaning one who displays inward beauty, not necessarily outward beauty. The apostle Peter said, 'Whose adorning let it not be that outward adorning of plaiting the hair, and of wearing of gold, or of putting on of apparel; but let it be the hidden man of the heart, in that which is not corruptible, even the ornament of a meek and quiet spirit, which is in the sight of God of great price. For after this manner in the old time the holy women also, who trusted in God, adorned themselves' (1 Peter 3:3-5)."

He flipped to the passage in a modern version of the Bible. " 'Your beauty should not come from outward adornment,' " he read, " 'such as braided hair and the wearing of gold jewelry and fine clothes. Instead, it should be that of your inner self, the unfading beauty of a gentle and quiet spirit, which is of great worth in God's sight. For this is the way the holy women of the past who put their hope in God used to make themselves beautiful.' "

He stared out the French doors, black with the night. "I want a woman with the unfading beauty of a gentle and quiet spirit."

"Lad, true beauty is unselfishness. Let me say here, pretty is as pretty does. If a girl is truly pretty, she will act pretty. In this old world of harshness and ugliness, it's a delight to find a girl who is interested in others. If she is kind to others, she will naturally be kind to her husband and her darling children, too."

Luke considered this. *Though the language is archaic, what the author is saying is true.*

"While I'm addressing beauty, I need to say a word here about her hair. The Bible says a woman's hair is her crowning glory. Do not go after girls with a manly bob or a shorn-to-the-scalp hairstyle that makes her look like a sheep on shearing day. Go after the girls with long, flowing, wavy hair."

Luke laughed.

"If a girl possesses inward beauty, that means she has the qualities of kindness, cheerfulness, patience, industriousness, and thriftiness. Lad, look into a girl's heart to find one like this. And when you find her, latch on to her and never let her go. Joybells will ring in your soul till death do you part."

I'm looking. I'm looking. He flipped to the next chapter, "Check Out the Little Things about Her."

"What does the inside of her house look like? If and when she invites you inside, take her up on it. However she keeps house now will be how she will keep house with you or some other lucky lad. Is the place neat and clean? Are the curtains starched and ironed? Does she live by the motto, 'A place for everything, and everything in its place'? If you are an organized person and you acquire a bride who is messy and slovenly, woe be unto you. The trials you will endure over this issue alone will be multitudinous. This is fair warning."

That's true.

"There are more little things you should consider. Happy is the lad who finds a bride who is a good companion. Perhaps she can ride a bicycle with you, or perhaps she's a bit fond of fishing, hunting, or outdoor life. Maybe she will read the same books as you and will be able to talk intelligently about them (though not too intelligently)."

Luke laughed so hard, his eyes misted over. When he stopped laughing, he flipped to another page. "Choosing a Wife Is Serious Business." *That's for sure.*

"God instituted marriage between a lad and a girl and expects it to last a lifetime. The marriage union is both physical and spiritual as you become one with your bride. For this reason, you must find a girl who will serve the Lord with you and pray with you, one who is involved in the Lord's work. That is of utmost importance. She must love the Lord her God with all her heart, soul, mind, and strength—just as you do. She must put Him first in her life."

I'm all for that. Luke closed the booklet. *That's always been at the top of my list.*

ten

Jeris came bounding out the side door of the church fellowship hall early Saturday morning, her arms loaded with picnic items. Audra followed closely behind, her arms full, too.

They made their way to the church van in the parking lot and packed the items in the back compartment.

"Here comes Blake." Audra shut the back doors of the van just as a car drove into the parking lot.

Jeris saw four more cars pull up near them. "And Jeffrey Phillips. And Patrice Edwards. And Denny Roper. Do you have a head count of the children? Didn't you say several of them are bringing friends or relatives?"

"Right. I think we're going to have nine children today."

"Isn't that great? Just think. We started with only three."

"God is using you to help build His kingdom, Jeris."

"I feel like it's a privilege to serve Him." She saw several children pile out of cars. "It's good you finally roped in Mrs. Edwards as a chaperone. I wouldn't want the two of us handling all these children at the beach."

"Didn't I tell you? She's not coming."

"She isn't? Then what are we going to do?"

"It's all taken care of."

"Who's helping us?"

Another car turned into the lot and parked. Luke Moore stepped out of the driver's side, and Brady bounded out of the backseat. Luke was dressed in shorts and sneakers.

"Luke?" Jeris was thunderstruck. "He's helping us chaperone?"

"That's right."

She tried to tamp down the chagrin inside her. She didn't like feeling this way, especially since her ill feelings were directed toward Audra Darling. The mere thought made her hurt inside. But she couldn't help it. "How? I thought you told me he turned you down."

Audra flashed her a mischievous smile. "The Lord works in mysterious ways, His wonders to perform."

ॐ

While Jeris gave pick-up instructions to the parents for when the party was over, Luke assisted Audra in corralling the children and securing them in seatbelts in the van.

Soon they were on their way, with Jeris driving. The children shouted and laughed and jumped on their seats as much as their seatbelts would allow. She was glad they were having a good time, but she wished they would calm down.

Luke sat in the front seat across the boxy console from her, but he was turned toward the back trying to establish order.

Audra, sitting on the bench seat behind Jeris, looked around and clapped loudly three times. "Children, quiet down."

The children ignored Audra's instruction.

Jeris had never seen them act like this. In her classroom there was occasional loudness, but nothing like this. It was the excitement of the party, she decided.

Even Audra's hot pink Fifi didn't do the trick. The children were simply too wound up.

Suddenly one child yelled as if in agony.

"Quit poking Denny, Jeffrey Phillips!" Audra called, near-exasperation in her voice. "I saw that. Keep your hands to yourselves. NBC. No bodily contact."

Luke, still turned toward the children, raised his arms in the air as if he were about to direct a choir. "Do-re-mi-fa-so-la-ti-do!" he belted out.

Every child grew quiet.

Jeris glanced at the kids through the rearview mirror and noted several had eyes as big as saucers.

"Do-ti-la-so-fa-mi-re-do," he sang backward. "Let's sing, kids." He smiled at them, his arms flailing in the air. He led them in a fast rendition of "Jesus Loves the Little Children" and then "The Wise Man Built His House upon the Rock," complete with hammering and raining motions.

The children followed his lead, apparently enthralled.

He led them in song after song.

Jeris noticed the songs were old, not the new praise songs she used in children's church. But that was okay. They were keeping the children entertained and still.

"These are the only kids' songs I know," he whispered to her between lyrics.

"They're doing the trick," she whispered back. "Keep it up."

Twenty minutes later she drove into the beach parking lot.

Luke hopped out, opened the long sliding door of the van, and put the step stool on the ground. He stood to the side at attention, as if he were an army sergeant, his hand in a salute position.

The first child climbed down the stool.

"Aye, aye." Luke saluted the little boy. "Line up here." He pointed to his left.

"Aye, aye." The boy saluted back and did as he was told.

Luke went through this procedure nine times until a long line of kids had formed.

Jeris and Audra were at the back of the van, loading their arms with picnic supplies. Jeris was glad for Luke's innovative control of the children.

Calling out military commands, he had them march to the back of the van. "March in place."

They obeyed, their little feet making *tap-tap-tap* noises on the pavement.

"Here," he said to Jeris, where she stood at the back compartment of the van. "Step aside and let me get the cooler. It's too heavy for you."

"Aye, aye, captain." She saluted him.

He saluted her back, then reached into the compartment and lifted out the cooler.

She had thought he was reserved and conceited but had to admit she was seeing a different side of him today. What did it matter, though, what she thought about him? Her thoughts or feelings about him would never amount to anything because she wouldn't let them. And neither would he.

"How did you dream up the military maneuvering?" she asked.

"It just came to me, I guess." He shrugged. "I was in ROTC in college."

"It's the Holy Spirit's illumination." Audra Darling nodded her head with a confident air.

&

Out on the beach, Luke set the cooler down in the sand under the shade of a palm tree. Like soldiers, the children marched in place behind him.

"Company, halt," he said as he faced them. "We're going to have a good time today, kids. But only if you obey orders. Is that understood?"

Nine "Yes, sirs" came out in unison.

He proceeded to lay down some rules. "No straying from the group. Obey the adults. Line up when you're told to. Come when you're called."

"We claim you as chaperone for every kids' outing," Audra said from behind him as the children waited quietly to be told what to do next.

He looked at her. "Very funny."

"I don't see anything funny about it, do you, Jeris?" Audra had an innocent look on her face.

Jeris was shaking out a blanket over the sand, the middle of it billowing up, then floating to the ground. "I think it's a Holy Spirit-illuminated idea."

Luke chuckled. He noticed Jeris wasn't wearing her usual bland clothing: the too-long skirts and the too-baggy jackets. Today she had on jeans that tastefully displayed her slenderness and a red shirt tucked in at her waist. She looked more casual and comfortable.

Jeris started the party with a vigorous game of dodge ball in the sand.

As they played, Luke watched Jeris, covertly, of course. He didn't want her to think he had bad manners. She seemed to come alive around the children. She was friendly and outgoing. And though she wasn't drop-dead gorgeous, she was pretty in an athletic and outdoorsy way. He liked that in her, something he'd never thought about in wife material.

Later, after one of the organized games, he watched her chase the children, catch them up in the air, and swing them around, laughing, as carefree as the wind. He recalled a few lines from the booklet he'd been reading, something about a lad being happy if his bride could ride a bicycle with him or was fond of the outdoor life.

He laughed out loud picturing June Cleaver in a fancy dress and pearls riding a bicycle beside Ward.

"What are you laughing at?" Jeris was out of breath from playing with the kids.

"Oh, nothing."

All morning he did what he could to be of help, and it looked as if his help was direly needed, as active as the children were. They waded in the water for a time, then picnicked on the blankets Jeris had spread on the sand.

After lunch she told them the story of Jonah, acting it out in front of them and applying the scriptural truths to their lives. Then she asked Luke to lead the kids in singing.

He was proud of himself when he remembered an old song from childhood, "Now Listen to My Tale of Jonah and the Whale." It was a perfect fit to her story.

After the singing, she announced it was time to hunt for sharks' teeth, and the kids squealed. Once they reached the place farther down the beach, she showed them how to hunt, raking her fingers through the sand. Soon the children were on their hands and knees, absorbed in their treasure hunting.

"Dad, Dad, I found one!" Brady came running up to Luke. He was hopping on both feet and grinning.

"Good going, Little Man." Luke hugged him. He examined the small, dark object in Brady's palm. "This is something you'll never forget, finding a shark's tooth on a Florida beach."

"This is the goodest time I ever had." Brady held the tooth in his tight little fist and waved it, smiling his ear-to-ear smile, his eyes dancing.

"It's been a fun day, hasn't it?"

Brady nodded, his cowlick sticking straight up.

"Which did you like best? Hunting for sharks' teeth? Playing games? Or the picnic with the—"

"The root beer?" Brady giggled.

Luke laughed. "You and your root beer. Let's see. What else did we do today? How about when we picked up seashells? Did you like that the best?"

"I liked the story Miss Jeris told us the very bestest. About Jonah and the whale."

Luke looked at the waves lapping at the shore. This was the ideal spot to teach the kids that particular story. "You liked that story the very bestest, huh?" He chuckled.

"Yes, sir. What's a *notion*, Dad?"

"A notion? Where'd that come from?"

"The song you sang about Jonah. Remember? You said Jonah had a very foolish notion."

"Oh. I guess you could say a notion is a way of thinking. And a foolish notion is a wrong way of thinking. God told Jonah to go to Nineveh, but Jonah didn't want to go, so he didn't obey."

"Kind of like when you come to Miss Jeris's class on Sundays and tell me it's time to go, but I don't want to leave?"

"You could say that, yes."

"Does everybody have foolish notions, Dad?"

Luke thought about it.

"Brady!" Jeris hurried over to them, smiling a Brady smile.

Enthusiasm laced her voice. "I hear you found a shark's tooth." She crouched in the sand next to Brady. "May I see it?"

"Yes, Miss Jeris." He opened his hand. "It was so fun."

Luke observed closely as Brady told her about the tooth and listened to her response. She was interested in Brady, as she was all of the children. It was apparent she loved the kids. And she interacted with them in an unusual way. It was a gift, something unique and special, he had to admit. He kept watching her as she talked with Brady. She took the tooth from his palm, held it up so it gleamed in the sunshine, and discussed Jonah and the whale with Brady.

"Brady," she said, "Jonah brought salvation to an entire town when he finally obeyed God."

Brady nodded. "That was the goodest story, Miss Jeris."

She laughed.

It was as if Luke were seeing her for the first time. *"Does everybody have foolish notions, Dad?"* Brady had asked. *I do, Brady,* he could've answered a few minutes ago. *I had a foolish notion that Jeris wasn't my type.*

Brady wrapped his arms around Jeris's neck. "Thank you for bringing us here today."

She hugged him back. "You're welcome, Little Man. I'm glad you had a good time. But, more than that, I hope some deep spiritual truths sank in here." With her index finger she touched his heart. "Maybe one day God will use you to help a lot of people see the light as Jonah did."

A warm feeling washed over Luke—a good feeling, an exciting feeling. *Brady, you certainly helped one person see the light. Me.*

eleven

"It's a good thing we left the beach when we did." Luke glanced across the console at Jeris, then stared at the deluge of rain hitting the windshield, the noise so loud it was almost deafening. "Who would've thought we'd get rain today?" He had to speak loudly to be heard. "With those cloudless blue skies we had at the beach?"

Jeris nodded as she gripped the steering wheel with both hands. "Typical of Florida, I guess. I'm glad it waited until now."

"Me, too." He looked down at his watch. Three thirty.

"The Lord gave us glorious weather for the party."

He nodded.

She tipped her head toward the rearview mirror. "Looks like the rain lulled them to sleep."

Luke glanced behind him. Most of the kids were sound asleep. Even Audra was leaning back against the seat, her eyes closed. "You two did a great job today."

"Thanks. You did, too. We appreciate your help."

He shrugged, feeling a little guilty he hadn't readily volunteered and in fact hadn't *wanted* to come when Audra first asked. Now he was glad he did. He liked the sense of fulfillment it gave him, to know he'd lent a hand to help in the Lord's work. The Lord's work? That's how the little booklet referred to church work. It said a man should find a wife who would serve the Lord with him, one who was involved in the Lord's work.

He glanced at Jeris again. She was certainly involved in the Lord's work. That was good.

The rest of the trip he didn't say any more, and neither

did she. He figured they were both a little tired after the full day. But he was looking forward to talking with her more, especially after the revelation hit him on the beach, the one Brady had brought him.

Soon Jeris pulled into the church parking lot. It was still raining heavily. She stopped the van under the wide carport beside the church. "It'll be easier to get the children out under here with the rain."

"Good idea." He unbuckled his seatbelt.

"Children, wake up," she called. "We're back."

Within ten minutes everyone had left the church except Luke, Brady, and Jeris. He offered to park the church van in its usual spot on the far side of the sanctuary. Then he dashed to his car, pulled up under the carport, and let Brady in.

Jeris thanked him again for his help, then ran through the rain to her vehicle.

As Luke drove through the parking lot on his way to the road, he noticed Jeris's vehicle hadn't moved out of her parking space. He backed up and pulled over beside her car. He tapped on his horn and inched his window down. She inched hers down. "What's the matter?" he asked.

"My windshield wipers won't work. I can't drive like this."

Rain was pouring into his car. "Can you make it to the carport?"

"I think so."

"Then come on." He closed his window and drove under the carport, leaving room for her to pull up beside him. "Stay inside, Brady." He hopped out of his car.

Brady was so sleepy that he didn't let out a peep.

Jeris got out of her car and stood there, the car pinging, with the key still in the ignition. She pulled out the key, and the pinging stopped. "I can't imagine what's wrong with the wipers. My SUV is brand-new."

"Some fluke thing, probably. It's under warranty, I'm sure."

She nodded.

"Leave it parked here, and I'll run you home. Then, when it quits raining, I can pick you up and bring you back to get it. On Monday you can take it to the dealership."

"I wouldn't want to impose—"

"You aren't imposing. Brady and I don't have any plans for the rest of the afternoon. It'd be no trouble at all."

"That's okay."

"But what else can you do? You can't drive in this downpour without windshield wipers."

"I could wait it out."

What was up with her? He was trying to be kind, and she was refusing it. Then he realized he was being forceful. "I'm sorry. I didn't mean to order you. I was only trying to be helpful."

"I—I. . ." Her voice trailed off.

"Let's start over. May I take you home and bring you back later?"

She shrugged. "Okay," she finally said.

❧

Luke opened the car door for Jeris, and she got in.

"Hi, Miss Jeris." Brady came alive. "I had the goodest time today." He rubbed the sleep out of his eyes.

"I did, too, Brady." She turned toward Brady and smiled, then gave Luke instructions on how to find her apartment.

Brady held up his shark's tooth. "I'm going to put this under my pillow tonight." His eyes were glowing, and he was smiling broadly, revealing his missing tooth.

She laughed.

Luke laughed, too. "Brady, that's for *your* teeth."

"Oh." Brady looked crestfallen.

"But maybe we can find a special place to display it."

Brady brightened.

"Maybe we can frame it and hang it in your bedroom."

"Yippee!"

After a few minutes Jeris gestured toward a large gated

apartment complex on her side of the highway. "Well, here we are. Take the next right."

Luke pulled into the complex. The buildings were painted in complementary hues that reminded him of a Florida sunset—corals, oranges, and burnished golds. Even through the steady rain he could see an architecturally pleasing clubhouse on the left and guessed a pool was behind it. Most complexes were built that way. Tennis courts were to the right. The landscaping design was superb. "Nice."

"Thanks. I enjoy living here." She fished in her purse. "Pull up to the gate, and you can swipe my card." She retrieved a thick white card from her purse and handed it to him.

He drove up to the huge black wrought-iron gate, lowered his window, and swiped the card. The gate opened in front of them. "Which way?"

"Follow this road a little ways, and I'll tell you where to turn when you come to my street." Within minutes she led him to her garage.

"These units have garages?" He was surprised. He knew this was a luxury complex, but he didn't realize they had garages. It had been a long time since he'd lived in an apartment.

"Some do." She pulled out a remote and clicked it, and the garage door opened. "Pull on in. A garage comes in handy for weather like this. That's why I chose this unit."

Luke drove in, turning off his wipers so they wouldn't flick water on the sides of the garage. A couple of tennis rackets hung on the wall above a bike.

June Cleaver surfaced.

He smiled inwardly.

Other than the bike and the tennis rackets, the garage was spotless.

Jeris opened her car door, then turned to him. "Thanks for the ride, Luke."

"Glad I was there when your mishap occurred." He put the car in REVERSE but kept his foot anchored on the brake.

"Me, too."

"Dad, I've got to go to the bathroom."

Jeris laughed, her eyes twinkling in delight.

"I keep trying to teach that boy manners." He rolled his eyes in a playful manner.

"Da–a–a–d—"

"We'll find a gas station on our way home, son."

"Bring him inside." She put her purse strap over her shoulder. "There's no need to hunt for a gas station in this deluge."

"I can't wait any longer, Dad."

Luke could only accept her kind offer. Secretly he was glad she had made it. He would get to spend a little more time with her. "Thanks, Jeris." He put the car in PARK and turned off the ignition.

"You're welcome. Come on in, guys."

"Do you have any root beer, Miss Jeris?" Brady undid his seatbelt and reached for the door handle.

"Brady." Luke rolled his eyes again.

"It's okay. It's no bother at all." She turned toward the backseat. "Yes, Little Man. I have some root beer."

"Yippee!"

&

Luke was curious as he walked into her apartment.

Brady darted across the room. He reached the hallway, stopped abruptly, and looked over at Jeris.

She gestured to the right. "Hurry, Brady. It's down the hall. At the end."

"Yes, ma'am." He ran like lightning, and the bathroom door slammed behind him.

Luke glanced around the tastefully decorated room.

"What does the inside of her house look like? If and when she invites you inside, take her up on it."

He squelched the chuckle roiling up inside as he re-membered Miss Ada's booklet again. He seemed to be doing that a lot today. It must mean it was sinking in. The author had said to check out the cleanliness and the neatness of Miss Possible's home.

Miss Possible? He smiled.

"Have a seat, Luke."

"Thanks." He sat down in an overstuffed leather chair that matched the sofa. *Nice.*

"Make yourself at home."

"I think I will." *I like the way that sounds.* He propped his feet up on the leather ottoman.

She crossed the room, stopped at an end table, and picked up a remote. She aimed it at the fireplace and punched a button, bringing up yellow flames on a bank of logs. She walked over and opened the glass doors. "This lets out heat. If you're as damp as I am, it'll probably feel good."

He settled back in the chair comfortably. The heat felt good, just as she'd said. But that wasn't what was making him feel as if he were walking on air.

She turned on a lamp, lit a candle on the coffee table, then sank into the leather sofa opposite him and rubbed her upper arms, making a *br–r–r* sound. "Oh, I forgot. Brady asked for a root beer." She jumped up. "Send him into the kitchen when he comes out, okay?"

"Sure." Luke watched her as she walked across the room and disappeared from sight. But he could hear her in the kitchen, scurrying about.

He looked around the pleasant room again. *You'd be very pleased, Mr. Granfield.* He smiled as he thought of the author of the booklet.

Luke felt pleased, too. The lamp, candle, and flames in the fireplace cast a luminous glow over the room. He admired the sophisticated brown leather sofa and matching chair, the accents of red in the sofa pillows, the flowing curtains at the windows, and the large painting over the sofa. The medium-colored wood of the end tables matched the TV armoire and the dining table he spotted in the alcove at the far end.

Brady came bounding into the room. "Where's Miss Jeris?"

"Did you wash your hands, Little Man?" Luke asked.

Brady saluted him. "Yes, Dad. Where's Miss Jeris?"

Luke stood up. "She's in the kitchen. Let's go find her." Hand in hand with Brady, he turned the corner and saw that the kitchen and dining area were one big room separated by a large island. Four stools with leather seats the color of her sofa were pulled up to the island. Another large painting with red and brown tones hung above a buffet on a far wall. *Nice,* he thought again.

"Miss Jeris, I like your house." Brady ran to her and gave her a hug where she stood near the stove.

She embraced him exuberantly. "Thanks, Little Man."

Finally he let go of her. He spotted a cage against the wall and raced to it. "What's this, Miss Jeris?"

"It's Sparky, my gerbil. He's my pet."

"You have a pet?" His eyes were round with wonder as he looked back at Luke.

She nodded. "I keep Sparky at my apartment on the weekends. But during the week he stays at my office."

"For the children you counsel?" Luke asked.

She nodded again, compassion in her eyes. "Sparky makes them feel more at ease. They seem to open up when they're holding him. They love him."

"Ooh," Brady said. "I love her, too. Can I hold her?"

"You mean *him*?"

"Yes, ma'am." Brady reached through the thin bars of the cage and touched the gerbil on the nose. "Please, Miss Jeris? Can I hold him?"

"Sure. Just be gentle."

"Maybe I'd better help." Luke stepped to the cage and knelt beside Brady, then opened the door. "Put your hand in here, Brady. Let Sparky smell you first."

"Are you a coffee or tea drinker, Luke?" She reached for two canisters on the counter and pulled them toward her.

"That sounds great." He smiled. "I could use a cup."

"You're not helping matters." She smiled back.

He laughed. "I'm game for either one. Really. Which is easiest?"

The teakettle on the stove whistled.

"Tea. You've already boiled the water."

She pulled the teakettle off the burner with a quick movement. "That doesn't matter. I can make coffee in a few minutes."

"That's all right. I'll take hot tea. Sounds good."

She nodded and pulled down two earthenware mugs, then gathered some more items, opening a cabinet door here or there.

"Can I pick him up now, Dad?" Brady ran his hand down the gerbil's back as far as the cage bars would let him reach.

"Okay. Just be careful, like Miss Jeris said." Luke was fascinated as Brady played with the gerbil. He'd begged for a pet for over a year, and Luke always told him they didn't have time for one. Maybe this was the answer. A gerbil. He'd have to ask Jeris how much care was involved. From the looks of things and by the way she talked about transporting the gerbil back and forth, it appeared this kind of animal might work for Brady.

"Luke? Brady? Are you ready for a snack?"

"Aw, Miss Jeris, do I have to put Sparky down now? I want to play with him some more."

"I have some cookies for you."

Brady kept playing with the gerbil.

Luke quickly washed his hands at the kitchen sink, then walked to the island. He was amazed at the spread she'd laid out. He'd been so absorbed in watching Brady with the gerbil, he hadn't noticed what she was doing. She'd put colorful dishes on coordinating placemats, and there was a box holding different types of tea bags. A plate held a variety of cookies on it, and a cheese board had two kinds of cheeses and crackers. At Brady's place she'd set a bottle of his favorite drink—root beer. Beside his plate were a few carrot sticks and a small wedge of fresh cabbage.

"Brady, come and eat your snack now," she said. "When you're finished, you can give Sparky a treat and play with him to your heart's content. Would you like to feed him?"

"Yippee!"

Luke sat down on the bar stool. "Put Sparky back in his cage, Brady, and go wash your hands."

"Yes, sir." Brady did as he was told this time.

In a few minutes the three of them were seated at the island. Jeris asked Luke to say the blessing.

He prayed, and when he opened his eyes, he saw on the counter a copy of a book the Sunday school class had recently studied. He gestured toward it. "How'd you like it?"

"It was thought-provoking. It's impacted a lot of lives, from what I've heard."

Luke took a sip of his hot tea, remembering Miss Ada's book. *"Maybe she will read the same books as you and will be able to talk intelligently about them (though not too intelligently)."*

He nearly choked on his tea, laughing. He grabbed his napkin and threw it across his mouth, still laughing.

Brady giggled. "What's so funny, Dad?"

Jeris put a small slice of cheese on a cracker. "I was wondering the same thing." Her voice had a drone effect, as if she were as interested as the man in the moon.

"Did Sparky make you laugh, Dad? Was it something he did?"

Luke looked across the room and saw Sparky staring at them from the cage, his mouth moving as if he were talking, his whiskers twitching up and down. "Sparky *is* funny, isn't he, Little Man?" Luke rubbed the top of Brady's head.

"You know, Dad"—Brady smiled brightly—"this is the goodest time I ever had."

۰

The rain finally stopped, and Jeris was grateful for the ride back to her car. After she arrived home she took a shower and dressed in comfy clothes, then sat down on the sofa. She turned on the TV but set it on MUTE. She had to do some mental housekeeping.

She hoped she'd managed to conduct herself in the way she'd intended while Luke was there. Her mind replayed everything she'd said and done. She'd been friendly. That was her nature. But she hadn't been too friendly. She'd been hospitable. That was her nature, too. But she hadn't overdone it. Cookies and cheese and crackers weren't too much, were they? Maybe she should've skipped the placemats and matching napkins. And her exuberance with Brady. But that couldn't be helped. She would never be distant with Brady, no matter how much space she wanted between her and Luke.

On and on the scene played in her head as she wondered about this and that. Had she been too harsh when she'd said parents needed to spend lots of time with their children, even if it meant cutting back their work hours? She'd half meant it as a slam against Luke but half meant it out of concern for Brady.

Other questions surfaced in her mind.

Until she felt troubled.

"This has to stop. No more. At least for tonight."

twelve

Jeris drove to the Hugheses' parsonage. Audra Darling had called her a couple of days ago and invited her to dinner tonight. She told her to come early so she could give her a few tips on making lasagna. The plan was to eat it as soon as they pulled it out of the oven. That sounded good to Jeris. She needed all the help she could get in the kitchen and had managed to leave work early.

She braked for a red light. A couple of weeks had passed since the beach party, and she'd stayed busy at work and church. Luke continued to drop Brady off at her children's church class, and he was friendly each time she saw him, though she wondered why.

Was it because of the beach party? Or his visit in her apartment? She was pretty sure he'd come out of his shell because of the visit. He'd called her a couple of times to get advice about gerbils. It seemed he was going to buy one for Brady. Both times he'd called, he'd lingered in conversation. Why, she didn't know. But she was glad Brady was getting a pet. It made children responsible. And gave them something more to love.

She pulled into the Hugheses' driveway and was surprised to see Luke's car. What was he doing here? He said he couldn't cook, so Audra was probably going to include him in the cooking lessons. But why did it have to happen on the same night she invited Jeris?

She bristled as she climbed out of her SUV, shut the door behind her, and walked to the front of the house.

Audra Darling welcomed her and gave her a hug, then led her into the kitchen.

Jeris felt herself clamming up as soon as she saw Luke.

"Hi, Jeris." He was leaning against a kitchen cabinet, his arms folded across his chest, looking like the handsome, self-assured man he was.

"Hi, Luke." Awkward. That's how she felt and wished she were a million miles away. She stopped at the table, put her hands on the back of a chair, and squeezed the maple wood. "Good to see you." *Sort of.*

"Same here. Looks like we're both getting cooking lessons tonight."

"It appears so." She let go of the chair, removed her purse from her shoulder, and set it on the table.

"I readily admit I need them," he said.

I do, too, but with you?

"Neither of you knows how to cook, so I decided to give you some tips tonight." Audra Darling tied an apron around her, nonchalance in her tone. "At the same time."

Jeris was on to Audra Darling's matchmaking. The children's beach party was her first hint. Before that, when she had invited them for Sunday dinner, Jeris hadn't given it a thought. But when Audra Darling had managed to get Luke to chaperone the party, she'd put two and two together. Now tonight—the lessons and dinner. With Luke. She knew Audra Darling was cooking up something.

And it's more than lasagna.

"Here, Luke." Audra Darling pulled out an apron from a lower kitchen drawer and placed it on the counter. "Put this on. It'll protect your shirt."

"Thanks." He put the apron over his head and smoothed out the folds in front.

Audra Darling took out another one. "And here's one for you, Jeris."

"Thanks." Jeris put on her apron, then reached behind herself and tied it.

Luke tried to tie his apron in back. "I need help. You have

to be a contortionist to do this."

Audra Darling laughed. "Jeris, can you help him?" Holding a large platter, she tipped her head toward Luke.

If I didn't love you to pieces, Audra Darling, I wouldn't like you right now. Jeris walked over to Luke as if she were a child going to the principal's office.

Luke turned his back to her, and while she tied his apron strings, he and Audra Darling chatted across the kitchen.

Jeris finished her task and moved away quickly.

Luke turned around. "Thanks, Jeris."

"You're welcome." She thought about Brady. "Where's Little Man?"

He pointed to the wide bank of windows over the kitchen table.

Brady stood on the low floating dock with Pastor Hughes, both of them holding fishing poles.

"Looks like they're having a good time." Jeris absently retied her apron.

"And so are we." Audra bustled about the large kitchen, taking things out of the refrigerator and the pantry and setting them on the counters.

Jeris strolled over to the windows, pretending to be interested in Brady and his fishing venture. But she wasn't. She was assailed with doubts about Luke. And about herself as she thought about what lay behind a good-looking man's face—the big ego thing. Wasn't that how it was? Weren't movie-star-handsome men macho and into themselves? Was it true or not?

thirteen

Jeris looked at her watch for the umpteenth time as she stood under the church carport. Eleven forty-five. "We've waited nearly thirty minutes. You think we ought to go ahead and leave? I don't think any more children are coming, do you? It looks as if we're only going to have three today."

Audra Darling shrugged her shoulders. "I thought an outing like this would've enticed a few more kids. Maybe it's too soon from our last outing. But that was a whole month ago."

Jeris nodded. Today they planned to take the children to the mall. First they would take them to Jolly Hamburgers for burgers and shakes and then to the kids' playground. After that, they would let them ride the new double-tiered merry-go-round in the center of the mall. Luke had volunteered to chaperone, and Jeris glanced at him sitting in his car with two little boys in the backseat beside Brady. She could see all three picking at each other and giggling.

"I have two church functions today." Audra Darling fished in her oversized shoulder bag. "One is a barbecue at the Winstons' home that starts at noon, and the other was this outing."

"*Was*? What's that supposed to mean?"

"I'm hoping you and Luke will agree to take the kids. Without me." She was still searching through her purse. "That way I can go on over to the Winstons'. I know it'll please them that I was able to come."

"Audra Dar—"

"They're celebrating Ned's sixtieth birthday. It's not just an ordinary come-have-lunch-with-us invitation." She pulled out a key ring full of keys. "They've invited tons of out-of-town family and friends, and they wanted to introduce Andrew and me to them as their pastors."

Jeris gave a resigned sigh. Audra Darling had a good reason to duck out of the kids' outing. But it would make things awkward. Luke was the last man she wanted to be stuck with. In the last few days—since Audra's cooking lesson—she'd spent some time sorting through her feelings, trying to make sense of her qualms, trying to weigh them and determine if there was any validity to them. She'd come to the conclusion that matters of the heart were almost too difficult to understand, even with her training in the field of psychology. Naturally Luke would be a good choice. He was a Christian and successful, but he wasn't her idea of—

"I take it by your silence you're in full agreement?" Audra Darling gave her a dazzling smile.

"I. . ." She nodded. What else could she do? What choice did she have? Audra Darling wasn't needed at the outing with only three children, but she *was* needed at Ned Winston's sixtieth birthday party. And Jeris would help her out. "Sure. Go ahead." She smiled. "But you'd better get a move on if you want to be on time."

"I knew you'd understand. You know how pastoring is. Everybody wants you." She was looking in her purse again. "I'll call Andrew and let him know I'm coming." She pulled out her cell phone and flipped it open. "And I'll go tell Luke my change in plans, okay?" She was already crossing the carport. She stopped and turned toward Jeris, her cell phone at her ear. "Jeris, you're a sweetheart."

"Who's a sweetheart?" Luke approached the carport. He wiggled his eyebrows.

Audra Darling threw her hand over her chest, whirled, and faced Luke. "Your deep voice startled me. I didn't know you were anywhere around. I thought you were still in your car."

"Sorry. I didn't mean to startle you. I came to see what the holdup is."

Audra Darling quickly explained the new plan to him.

"That's fine with me," he said. But he wasn't looking at Audra Darling. He was looking at Jeris. Intently.

Jeris dropped her gaze to the concrete. She had too much to think about concerning him. "Do you want to take your car or mine, Luke?"

❧

Luke marveled at Jeris from where he sat on the parklike bench on the first tier of the merry-go-round. He'd thought she was. . .gray. That was what he'd called it after he first met her. But she wasn't gray at all. She was pink and lavender— carefree and uninhibited. She'd shrieked like a child when they first walked up to the new merry-go-round, which made the boys shriek, too. Instead of the usual horses and tigers and zebras, this merry-go-round had sea animals. Dolphins. Seals. Seahorses. Manatees. Whales.

She'd jumped onto a dolphin and started humming the theme song to the old TV show *Flipper*, making the boys laugh.

She was all smiles and laughter, not her usual quiet self. She'd seemed inhibited every time he'd been around her, except for the children's beach party when she'd been playful and friendly like today. The children definitely brought it out in her, and he liked it.

Could *he* bring out those same qualities in her? If he could, maybe he would get to know her better.

❧

That evening Luke and Brady ate a soup-and-sandwich supper, then swam in the pool until dark. Afterward Luke fixed Brady a snack while Brady took his bath. Later he read him a book, prayed with him, and tucked him in bed.

"Good night, Little Man." Luke kissed him on the forehead. "I love you."

"I love you, too, Dad. And I love Audra Darling. And I love Pastor Hughes." He named six or seven other people he loved. "And I love Gerbil."

"Are you still calling him Gerbil?" Luke had laughed when Brady insisted on naming him Gerbil after he bought him at the pet store. But he'd let Brady do what he wanted. It was his pet.

"That's his name, Dad."

"Okay. If you say so."

"You know who I love almost as much as I love you, Dad?"

"Who's that?"

"Miss Jeris."

Luke wasn't surprised. He knew Brady enjoyed spending time with Jeris. He was always asking about her. "Well, sleep tight, Little Man." He kissed him on the forehead again.

"Yes, sir."

Luke closed the door behind him and walked into the family room. He saw Miss Ada's booklet on the end table. He hadn't read it in a while. He supposed it was time to pick it up again.

He plopped down on the sofa, comparing it to Jeris's leather one, thinking maybe he'd enjoy a sofa like hers. Hers was much more attractive than his. She definitely had good taste in furnishings.

He reached for the booklet and flipped to a new chapter: "Why You Need Marriage."

"Marriage is a companionship, a blending of two souls before God. It is right and fitting and good that a lad should have a wife and that a girl should have a husband.

God brought the first couple together, Adam and Eve. In Genesis chapter one, we see that as God created the heavens and the earth, He saw each thing that He created was good. Six times the Bible says God saw that it was good.

But it is significant to note that when God created man in the recording of chapter two, He said (not saw), 'It is not good that the man should be alone; I will make him an help meet for him.'

God knew it wasn't good for Adam to remain alone. He needed a wife. So God set about creating Eve for him. Then he presented her to Adam, and the Bible says, 'Therefore shall a man leave his father and his mother, and shall cleave unto his wife: and they shall be one flesh' (Genesis 2:24).

Lad, you need a wife.

You need a wife to cleave to.

You need a wife to be one flesh with."

Amen to that. Luke wiggled his eyebrows, smiling from ear to ear.

"And as I've stated before, you need God's choice of a wife. She must be the right one. Rest assured, she's out there, lad, reserved just for you. Your job is to seek the Lord about her, and the Lord's job is to speak to her heart about you."

Luke paused from his reading and bowed his head. "Lord, I'm trying to seek You about this matter. I know it'll take a special woman to agree to a marriage with a child thrown into the deal. But You know just who I need. And You know just who Brady needs. I choose to believe she's out there. And, Lord, if it's Jeris, please soften her heart toward me. In Jesus' name. Amen."

fourteen

Jeris looked across the table at Carrie Denton, the office manager she'd hired when she opened her practice. Carrie was doing a great job, and she couldn't be more pleased with her work. She was thankful for this new friend, what she'd asked God for when she moved to Silver Bay. Though they didn't attend the same church, Carrie was a believer, and Jeris had enjoyed their friendship. She also enjoyed the short time they shared each morning before the workday began, when they prayed for God's blessings and for the troubled children Jeris counseled.

"What time do you have to be at the airport in the morning, Jeris?"

"My plane leaves at eight, so I'd like to get there around six thirty."

"Then I need to pick you up at six, right? Will that give us enough time?"

"Plenty. Saturday morning traffic is nothing compared to weekdays."

Carrie nodded. "That's for sure."

"Thanks for offering to take me."

"You're welcome. And·I'm to pick you up late Sunday night, right? After you get back from the conference? At 10:30?"

"If you don't mind. I really appreciate your help."

"You're welcome again."

Jeris smiled. "I hate missing my children's church class on Sunday, but Audra Darling said she'd cover for me. Remember I told you about her? My pastor's wife?"

Carrie nodded. "I'd like to meet her sometime. Anybody with a name like that—well, I'd just like to meet her."

"She's a neat person. A charming, Southern lady." Jeris took a sip of her sweet iced tea. "Where's Martin this time?"

"Miami again."

"When will he be back?"

"Saturday night. I can't wait for him to get home. I've missed him like crazy this week."

"Typical sentiments of newlyweds."

"I'm having a hard time dealing with Martin traveling so much. Thanks for meeting me for dinner tonight. I hate eating alone, don't you?" A stricken look crossed her face. "I'm sorry. I should think before I speak. I didn't mean to be insensitive. I wasn't even thinking about. . .about your eating alone all the time. Oh, my. I'm bungling this."

"It's all right. Don't worry about it." Jeris smiled to make Carrie feel better. "I've been eating alone so long that I never think twice about it." She laughed. But her laugh felt hollow.

Carrie stared down at her plate. "Jeris?" She looked up. "I've been praying about something. . .something for you."

Jeris could feel it coming. Was she going to say she'd been praying God would send Jeris a husband? It didn't offend her if that was the case. On the contrary she wanted all the prayers she could get.

"I've been asking the Lord to send a special man into your life."

"Then that makes two of you praying for that."

"Two?"

"Audra Darling told me she's praying the same way."

"Then why don't you make it *the three of us*?"

"Three?"

Carrie wagged her finger at her. "You need to be joining in this prayer."

Jeris shrugged. "God knows my heart. I suppose if it's meant to be, it'll happen."

"But He wants us to pray in specific ways."

"I guess so."

"And you know what else He wants?"

"What's that?"

"He wants us to be open to *His* plans. Sometimes His ways are not our ways."

"Meaning?"

"Well, for instance, what if God has a beta male in mind for you?"

"Beta? I've never heard the term. I know sanguine and choleric and melancholy and phlegmatic—you know, the personality types. And then there're the Briggs-Meyer classifications. But *beta*?"

Carrie held up a bookstore bag, then laid it on the table. "I stopped by the bookstore on my way here and bought a book. It's about heroes and heroines in romance novels and—"

"How's your writing coming along?" Jeris took a bite of her chicken alfredo.

"I just finished chapter four of my novel. If I write a page a day, I figure I can finish it in about four or five months. That class I told you about—the one I'm taking at the community college every Tuesday night? I'm learning a lot about fiction writing. The instructor is a published author of twelve novels."

"Wow."

"She's been teaching from this book the past couple of weeks." Carrie touched the bag. "I'm going to highlight the things she's teaching so I can learn it."

"Just remember me when you're rich and famous."

Carrie laughed and rolled her eyes, her long dark eyelashes fluttering. "Right, right."

"I'm serious."

"Right, right." She pulled the book out of the bag. "This author says there are two types of heroes. The alpha and the beta."

"And the beta is—?"

"He's the one we don't want to read about in novels, according to the author and according to my instructor. The beta hero is the soft-spoken, supersensitive, easily led gentleman."

Jeris thought about her balding, bookish man. "That's the kind of man I'm looking for. That type of guy is tender, at least from what I've observed. And that's the number one thing I want in a man. Tenderness."

"But what if God wants to give you an alpha male?"

"And what are alpha males?"

"That's basically what this book is all about. The alpha male is described as a strong, powerful man."

"Sounds pretty good to me, too." Jeris giggled.

"They can be tough and hard and arrogant and macho."

She frowned. "No, thanks."

Carrie opened the book, ran her finger down a page, and flipped to the middle of the book. "This says, 'Romances are stories of strong women taming dominant men.'"

"I'll pass on the domination thing."

"It says, 'The heroine needs a hero who's a formidable challenge to her.'"

"Not my cup of tea."

"Have you ever read *Jane Eyre*?"

"It was one of my favorite books when I was a teenager."

"Okay, there's an alpha male."

Jeris ran a slice of Italian bread through the oil-and-herbs mixture on her bread plate, then took a bite. She savored the flavors, recalling the story she'd always loved, the tale of the plain though noble heroine Jane and the dashing though distant Mr. Rochester. She thought about Mr. Rochester, scenes of him and Jane playing in her head as if they were on a movie screen.

"This says, 'The alpha hero can be unlovable *at first*.'"

Jeris sipped her tea, thinking about Jane Eyre's alpha hero. "Mr. Rochester was like that."

"Right. He didn't reveal his vulnerability—"

"Or his true character—"

"Until the end." Carrie nodded her head vigorously. "Here's

a second story like that one—*Beauty and the Beast*."

Jeris nodded. "Another unlovable hero—"

"*At first*. Those are important words. This book says, 'The alpha hero has the capacity to finally temper his toughness and, in so doing, to love the heroine passionately and faithfully.'"

Jeris let out a sigh. It would be wonderful to find a strong, intelligent, successful man like Carrie was talking about and fall deeply in love with him and him with her. He could be brash at first like Mr. Rochester or the Beast, but his loving nature would finally win out, and all would be utopia.

"'The alpha hero is a powerful man who finds out his life isn't complete unless he wins the hand of the heroine,'" Carrie read.

Suddenly Jeris's practical side surfaced like a diver out of oxygen. Carrie wasn't talking about reality. She was talking about fantasy. Pure and simple.

"This says, 'During the course of the novel, as the heroine comes to trust the hero, the hero comes to trust her, true love wins out, and they live happily ever after.'"

"You forget one thing." Jeris tried to keep a hard edge out of her voice.

"What's that?"

"I'm no heroine in a novel."

Carrie shut the book. "Of course not. I know that. What I'm trying to get you to see is, don't box God in."

"How do you know I'm doing that?"

"I don't know that you are. I just care about you and want to see you as happily married as I am. And that's achieved by not boxing God in. . .by letting Him work as *He* wants to work so He can send you the man *He* wants for you. Sometimes single women are single for a reason. They get too picky and too hard to please. They put all the emphasis on what they want and not on what God wants. It's as if they're putting parameters on God's will—"

"How could you know that?"

"Because that's how I was before I met Martin. I've been down this road. I speak from experience. I was looking for the complete opposite of Martin. I knew what I wanted and thought it was all about that. Now he's the love of my life. But when I first met him I wouldn't give a chewing-gum wrapper for him. Then we sort of grew on each other, and Cupid's arrow pierced our hearts."

Carrie touched her heart and fluttered her long dark eyelashes. Then her brows drew together contemplatively. "No, the heart of the matter is, God had it all planned out that we would fall in love and marry. I just had to be open to Him."

Jeris had a lot to think about. Her balding, bookish man might not be God's plan for her, and a little flutter of fear gripped her heart. That image had been a comfort to her for a long time.

"You can trust in the Lord, Jeris."

"I've been a Christian nearly all my life. I fully understand that."

"Do you really?" Carrie gave her an unwavering stare.

Jeris looked down, studying her nails. In psychological terms, she knew she had "trust issues."

"He wants the best for you. You don't have to be afraid."

"Who said anything about being afraid?"

"I did." Carrie gave her that unwavering stare again. "The first step to conquering a problem is admitting there is one."

"Hey, who's the psychologist here?" Jeris smiled wryly. "You should get your license."

"I'm sorry." Carrie's face flushed. "I just want to help."

"Thanks," Jeris said in a deadpan voice.

fifteen

Jeris walked briskly down the hall after children's church was over, thinking about the kids. She'd enjoyed being with them this morning. She'd missed them last Sunday when she was away at the conference. She made her way through the side door of the sanctuary. Audra Darling would be along momentarily—she'd stayed in their classroom to see the last child picked up.

Now that morning service was over, they were going to pack away the puppets in the sanctuary and take down the portable puppet stage they'd set up yesterday. Pastor Hughes had asked their class to do a short puppet show at the beginning of the service this morning, and it had been a rousing success. The congregation thoroughly enjoyed the program as the children worked the puppets to a backdrop of lively kids' praise music. And it had produced some visitors. Several people who normally didn't attend church—parents and grandparents of the new children—had come to see their kids perform.

She walked up the steps to the platform and over to the puppet stage. She stepped behind the heavy purple curtains hanging from white plumbing pipes and picked up Mrs. Mizelle Mouse, then placed her in the packing box. She put Mr. Billy Bear beside her, gathered more of the puppets, and packed them away, fitting them deftly into the box.

Audra Darling joined her behind the curtains. "I'm glad you had a good trip last weekend, Jeris. I'll tell you what, those kids missed you like crazy." She picked up Miss Erma Elephant and placed her in the packing box.

"I missed them, too. I hated to be away. But it couldn't be helped. I'm just glad I had you to take care of my class."

110

"Luke served as my assistant."

"Really?" Jeris heard Brady in the sanctuary. His chirpy little voice echoing in the vaulted ceiling announced his presence.

"Can I lend a hand?" came Luke's voice.

Audra Darling pulled the curtains apart and stuck her head through the opening. "Sure. Come on up."

"Come on, Brady. Let's go up onstage."

"Yippee!"

Jeris tugged on the curtains and pulled them back farther so she could see out. In a little while they would unscrew the white plumbing pipes from the joints and work the curtains completely off and fold them.

Luke and Brady walked down the aisle and up onto the platform.

"Can I go behind the curtains, Dad?"

"No, son. We don't need you to get in the way. We have to take the stage down. We'll be finished soon. Just sit on that chair over there." He pointed to a high-backed, red upholstered oak chair that stood near the pulpit.

"Aw, Dad." Brady climbed up on the big chair, his little legs dangling.

Luke approached the puppet stage and started unscrewing the joints.

Jeris smiled at Brady and motioned for him to come to her.

Brady hopped off the chair, ran to the puppet stage, and joined her.

She turned to Luke. "I'm sorry." She realized her mistake too late. "I should've asked you first. Is it okay if Brady helps me pack the puppets?"

"You sure he won't get in the way?"

"Please, Dad." Brady held his hands under his chin in his familiar prayer stance.

"Of course he won't. I'll put him to work." She nuzzled Miss Ollie Ostrich under Brady's chin, and he squealed like a banshee.

"Okay, Little Man, you can help Miss Jeris."

For nearly twenty minutes they all worked, packing the puppets, taking down the plumbing pipes, folding the heavy curtains, and putting them and the pipes into the boxes.

"Done." Jeris ran her fingers in a zigzag trail down Brady's back. "Good job."

"Thanks, Miss Jeris."

"Brady, why don't you quote last Sunday's memory verse for Miss Jeris?" Audra Darling winked at Jeris. "It'll prove I taught you tykes something while she was gone."

"Yes, ma'am." Brady walked over to the edge of the platform. He put his little heels together and stood statue still, staring out at the sea of empty pews as if they were filled with parishioners. " 'Man looks at the outward appearance,' "—he said it in a singsong, little-boy style—" 'but the Lord looks at the heart.' First Samuel 16:7."

"Good job again, Brady." Jeris made her way to him, feeling proud of him. All children needed to learn the scriptures, and Brady had memorized quite a few. "You're a smart boy."

"Good going, Little Man," Luke said.

Brady thrust his hands straight out to his sides, hummed the theme to *Batman*, and made a flying leap off the platform.

"Oh, my." Jeris took a deep gulp. The platform was high.

Brady landed on the carpeted area in the space behind the altars.

"Brady!" Luke ran down the steps, worry in his voice.

Jeris hurried down the steps, too.

Luke reached him first. "Son, don't ever do that again. You could've been hurt." He looked him over closely, checking his arms and legs. He touched the top of his head. "Does anything hurt?"

"No, sir."

Concerned, Jeris bent down, touched Brady's upper arm, and gave it a feathery stroke as she looked up at Luke. "Are you sure he's okay?"

Luke nodded. "I'm sure." He chuckled. "I checked out his outward appearance, though only God can see the inside."

❧

As he drove to Dale's Café for lunch, Luke thought about the verse Brady quoted. His son was doing it again. He was helping Luke see the light. With a hurtful pang he recalled the prejudice he'd had toward Jeris when he first met her.

But his hurt eased when he remembered the prayer he'd prayed and how God had answered it. *Please prepare my heart. Whatever needs changing in me, please do it. I'm open and willing.*

He smiled as he drove along, thankful the prejudice had long been plucked from his heart. *Thank You, Lord, for answering my prayer.*

Tenderly he thought of Jeris and her endearing ways. Not only was she beautiful outwardly but she also had a beautiful heart, what Miss Ada's booklet talked about.

"And it's a heart I want to win."

❧

Jeris pulled down the covers of her bed and crawled in. The children she'd been counseling lately in her office popped into her mind. Tough situations that needed the wisdom of Solomon. Three children acting out hostilities following divorces. A rebellious teenager driving her parents crazy. A child slowly going bald and her family not knowing why. But Jeris thought she knew. Friday the little girl had finally told her about the bully at school who'd been threatening her the entire year.

Jeris pushed back the covers and slipped to her knees, remembering Jesus' words in the Bible, His instructions for situations that seemed impossible. *These kinds of problems can be resolved only with prayer.* For several minutes she beseeched the Lord to help the children she counseled and to give her godly wisdom in dealing with them.

"Lord, give me Your words to say as I counsel them, not my words and not some textbook jargon. Help me to give them the living words, the words of life, the words of You, Lord."

She finished praying and climbed back in bed, then reached for her Bible and devotional on her nightstand. It was her pattern every night to read the devotional and the scripture it talked about, then ponder them. She reached for a novel, too. Since she wasn't sleepy she would read for a while when she finished her devotions. Reading always made her drowsy.

As she repositioned her pillows she thought of the novel *Jane Eyre*, the story she and Carrie had talked about. She remembered Carrie's questions about the alpha and beta heroes. Alpha? Beta? Wasn't Pastor Hughes a beta man? He was kind and gentle and compassionate and caring. That's what she wanted in a man. But wait a minute. Wasn't he a take-charge person, too? A strong man with a backbone of steel? She wanted those attributes, too, in a husband. She wanted a man who could sum up a situation quickly and do something about it—a "change agent" the newspaper had called it in a story she'd read about people who made a difference in the lives of others. *But*—the word loomed big in her mind—her future husband had to be tender.

She was confused. Alpha or beta? Beta or alpha? Which did she want?

She flipped open the devotional book and turned to today's date.

"I can't believe this." The devotional featured the scripture Brady had quoted in the sanctuary today, right before he took that flying leap off the platform. She smiled, remembering his Batman antics.

" 'Man looks at the outward appearance, but the Lord looks at the heart,' " she read, awed by the coincidence. Hadn't someone said a coincidence was when God didn't get the credit?

But God *would* get the credit for this. She repeated the verse and let it sink in, then slipped out of bed and dropped to her knees again. "Lord, thank You for putting this scripture before my eyes twice today. You must want me to take it to heart. Your Word is living and true, and it speaks to us just when we need it."

She recalled Carrie's encouraging her to pray about God sending the right man into her life. "Lord, I recognize through this verse You're saying You know what's best concerning a husband for me. You can look into his heart, and I can't. All I can see is the outside. Help me to be open to You and Your plan. Forgive me for wanting my own way. Help me to trust You wholly and completely, with no fear or doubt or worry but with a full confidence that You know best and have my life planned out."

She continued pouring out her heart to the Lord. "I submit myself to you." She took a deep breath, the very act seeming to fill her soul with confidence. God's confidence. "I don't care if the man I marry is bald or ugly or handsome or tall or short. Or whatever. I put my trust in You to lead and guide me to the right one. In Jesus' name. Amen."

She climbed back in bed. But this time she didn't reach for a book. Instead she turned off the light and fell asleep as peacefully as Job must have after his restoration.

sixteen

"I have something to tell you, Audra Darling." Bent over a little girl at the activity table, Jeris glanced up at Audra Darling, then looked back down and picked up a blue crayon. She colored part of the sky on the little girl's color sheet. The child needed encouragement. One of the boys had made fun of her coloring last week, and today she'd refused to participate in the activity. "See what I'm doing, Charity? It's so much fun to color." She put the crayon in Charity's hand. "You try it now."

Charity colored part of the sky, not going out of the lines once.

Jeris smiled at her, then tweaked her button nose. "Good job, Charity. Keep it up, and soon your whole sheet will be colored. Isn't it fun to color?"

"Yes, ma'am."

Jeris stood up and pushed the arms of her jacket up to her elbows. Though she liked the professional look this type of suit gave her, she liked being free from long sleeves when she did activities with the children. Maybe she could find a short-sleeved version of this jacket. She would look in her favorite clothing catalog when she went home.

"I have something to tell you, too, Jeris." Audra Darling whisked over to the metal cabinet, opened the door, and pulled out another box of crayons. She made her way back to the activity table and plunked the crayons down in the middle. "Something important."

"What?"

Audra Darling gestured at the children. "When they leave."

Jeris nodded her agreement. They would talk later when

they could concentrate. She looked forward to telling Audra Darling about her trust issues and how the Lord had helped her with them.

All morning they worked with the children, coloring, telling Bible stories, singing praise songs along with CDs, supervising free playtime. Jeris wondered what Audra Darling wanted to tell her. She knew what *she* wanted to say to Audra Darling.

When the last child left, Jeris and Audra Darling cleaned up the room.

"Do you have lunch plans?" Audra Darling pushed the last chair under the table, then picked up her purse and Bible.

"You're not inviting me to your house again. You do that too much, and I don't want to take advantage."

"I've told you over and over. When I invite you, it's because we really want you to come. But don't worry about that right now. I didn't cook today. Andrew's out of town."

"That's right." Jeris remembered. He'd gone on a free trip to Israel for pastors only, and the assistant pastor had preached in the service today. "When's he coming back?"

"End of the week. I wish I could've gone. I've always wanted to see Israel. But he's planning to put together a trip for our church people the first of next year, and I'll get to go on that one."

"That'll be great." Jeris followed Audra Darling to the door of their classroom. They stepped into the hall, and Jeris closed the door behind them.

"Maybe we could grab a sandwich somewhere? And talk?"

"Sounds good." Jeris walked beside Audra Darling down the long hall.

"Where?"

Audra Darling named a restaurant.

"See you there."

෨

"Okay. So what did you want to tell me?" Jeris took a bite of her pita sandwich, noting how good the blend of chopped apples and chicken tasted.

"You tell me first." Audra Darling put down her sandwich—the same kind Jeris was eating—and took a sip of her fruit drink. "Did you taste the apples in this chicken salad? I'm going to have to try adding them the next time I make it."

"Yes, I did. Delicious. You tell me first what you wanted to say."

"All right." Audra Darling took another sip of her drink, looking as serious as she'd ever looked. "I'm not sure how to say this. . . ."

"You? Miss Talkative-at-the-Drop-of-a-Hat? You don't know what to say?"

"I said *how*. Not *what*. Okay. I won't beat around the bush. I think you and Luke Moore are made for each other."

"That's not surprising. You've been matchmaking ever since I moved here."

"Has it been that obvious?"

"For me it has." Jeris smiled, slowly shaking her head and giving Audra Darling a shame-on-you look. Then something hit her. Luke had probably noticed Audra Darling's matchmaking, too. She could feel her face growing warm. Did he think she'd put Audra Darling up to it? She hoped not.

"I think he's the one for you, Jeris." Audra Darling plunged in, telling Jeris about Al and Gloria Stanfield and how she'd arranged some times for them to be together, including dinner at her house. Within a few months the love bug hit, she said, and they got married and now lived in wedded bliss.

"Wedded bliss?" Jeris smiled. It was an old-fashioned term, but it intrigued her. In fact it sounded enticing. And comforting.

"Somehow I knew they were meant for each other. I feel like the Lord used me to get them together. But, Jeris, that was the first time I ever did anything like it. It's not my usual way. But a strong feeling seemed to come over me with both

Al and Gloria, and now with you and Luke. Of course, we have to wait and see how it works out, and maybe I'm wrong about you two, but somehow I knew about Al and Gloria."

"Holy Spirit illumination?" Jeris smiled her brightest.

"You could say that."

Neither said anything for a long moment, as if what had been uttered needed time to germinate in the soil of a heart— Jeris's.

Finally Jeris broke the silence. "What do you think I should do about what you've just told me? I mean, if it's the Lord's plan, this is like a secret knowledge I'll have about us. How am I supposed to deal with it?"

Audra Darling smiled. "That's a typical question from a psychologist."

"*This* psychologist needs some answers."

"It's simple. Be open to God."

That sounded familiar. "That's what I wanted to talk to you about."

"Oh?"

Jeris plunged in this time, detailing everything that had happened to her recently, from her conversation with Carrie to Brady's scripture verse to her prayer. She told Audra Darling how she'd poured out her heart to the Lord. She described how she'd relinquished her cares to Him. "I even told the Lord I don't care *what* the man I marry looks like." She laughed, feeling as light as a seagull's feather.

"That's part of God's plan, Jeris, in all of this. Your relinquishment."

Jeris nodded. She felt her eyes misting over. "He can be tall or short or bald or good-looking or ugly. . .or whatever. It doesn't matter anymore. What matters is if he's the one. . .the Lord has for me." A tear escaped down her cheek. "It's a big thing for me to be able to say that."

Audra Darling reached across the table and patted Jeris's hand in a motherly gesture. "I know."

Jeris smiled. "More Holy Spirit illumination?"

Audra Darling nodded. "Everything's going to work out. In God's timing." She paused, her eyebrows drawn together. "When—and not if—Luke asks you out, be prepared."

The thought was thrilling to Jeris. Even if he was as handsome as a superstar.

ॐ

As Jeris got in her car and buckled her seatbelt, she was enjoying the feelings of anticipation washing over her.

"'Anticipation,'" she sang, an old song her mother liked to hum. Audra Darling said Luke *would* ask her out. She'd advised her to be prepared when it happened. Well, she would be.

A knock sounded at the car window.

She was so deep in thought that she nearly jumped. She looked up, saw Audra Darling, and punched her window button.

"Sorry—I didn't mean to startle you," Audra Darling said through the open window. "Are you free this coming Saturday?"

"Why?"

"I have something in mind. Can you check your schedule?"

Jeris took out her pocket calendar, studied it, then looked up. "I'm free. What are you thinking?"

"There's a new mall in Tampa, and I was wondering if you could go shopping with me. We could do an all-day girl thing, you know, shop, eat lunch in a nifty place, shop some more, take our time, enjoy ourselves—"

"It sounds like fun. I'll shop with you, but I don't need to buy anything. I'm about to order a few business pieces from *Officebound* catalog."

"You never know." Twinkles danced in Audra Darling's eyes. "Hold off on your ordering."

seventeen

Luke sat on a wicker chair on his lanai late Thursday afternoon, watching Brady at the shallow end of the pool. He also kept an eye on the hamburgers on the grill.

Hamburgers.

The last time he'd chaperoned Brady's children's church outing, he and Jeris had taken the kids to Jolly Hamburgers for burgers and shakes.

He'd been thinking about her a lot lately. Every time he'd been with her, she'd maintained a stiff persona. At least with him. With Brady and the kids in her class, she brightened like the Florida sunshine. But with him she'd maintained a reserved front at all of their encounters.

He picked up Miss Ada's booklet and turned to another chapter: "What Dating Can Do for You."

"Dates can be useful, in that dates provide the venues for relationships to be explored. It goes without saying that the lad should be a gentleman on dates. He should act honorably, and likewise, the girl should act in the same manner. NBC. From the outset, No Bodily Contact should be your rule."

Luke hooted. That was the term Audra Darling had used when the kids picked at and punched each other in the van. He thought it was funny then, and it was funny now.

"Dating should not be looked on as the only method of finding a wife. But it can be of help. Though you won't see every side of the girl's behavior while on dates, if you keep your wits about you, you will be able to determine a great deal. You will observe her in many situations, and thus you can decide whether she has the attributes that are needed to make a good wife."

Luke didn't know what to think. This sounded so. . .so what? All he could think of was a hawk watching its prey. He wasn't a hawk, and a date wasn't a prey. But in a way the author was right. After all, marriage was serious business. It was forever. And it needed careful consideration.

"On a first date, you can decide if you are interested in her enough to pursue further dates. If you are, then ask her out again."

That makes sense.

❧

"Watch me, Dad." Brady's shrill voice echoed across the aqua blue pool water. "I'm going to stand on my hands, and this time I'm going to hold my breath for sixty minutes."

"You mean sixty seconds?"

"Look, Dad."

"Okay, Brady." Luke put the booklet down on the table. "Stand on your hands. I'm looking. I won't take my eyes off of you, Little Man."

Brady went down headfirst into the water and stood on his hands, his little feet barely above the water level. In seconds— but longer than he'd ever stayed down before—he surfaced. "I did it, Dad, didn't I?"

"You stayed down a long time. Good going, son. Keep practicing. It's good for your lungs."

Brady went down headfirst again, then resurfaced.

Luke picked up the booklet.

"When you decide to date a certain girl, make a mental

checklist of everything she does. First of all, does she accept the date with coquettishness?"

Coquettishness? What an old-fashioned word. "Sit on the first step, Brady. I need to go inside for a sec."

"Aw, Dad."

"Now, Brady."

"Yes, sir." Brady did as he was told.

Luke dashed inside—the booklet still in his hand—found his dictionary, and hurried back out. "Okay, Brady. You can get in the water now."

Brady jumped in the pool and splashed about.

Luke sat down, paged through the dictionary and came to *coquette.* "That's close enough. 'A woman who endeavors without sincere affection to gain the attention of men.'"

He picked up the booklet again and decided to reread the portion he'd just read before continuing on.

"When you decide to date a certain girl, make a mental checklist of everything she does. First of all, does she accept the date with coquettishness? Or sincerity? Is she agreeable to your plan, or does she insist on hers? Is she punctual or late? (It's okay for her to be a tiny bit late some of the time.)"

Luke chuckled.

"While on the date, is she kind to those around her? Does she treat people with respect? Does she display good manners? Notice these things carefully. Does she order the most expensive thing on the menu, or is her choice conservative? (This will tell you how she'll be as a wife. Need I say here that frugality is your goal?)"

I don't care what a woman orders. If I'm taking her out, I want her to order whatever she likes. I'm no Scrooge.

"Do you feel good in her presence? Does she talk a lot? Too much? Does she have the tendency to talk the hind legs off a donkey?"

Luke laughed hard. This author had a way with words.

"A girl needs to be a good conversationalist on many topics (but not too many topics)."

Oh, brother. Here we go again.

"Does she conclude the date with a sincere thank-you? Does she dally while saying good-bye? If she dallies, does she toy with your affections? Does she try to hold your hand on the first date (horrors!)? If so, run from this girl, and never date her again!"

"Dad, I smell something burning."

Luke jumped up and dashed to the grill, the booklet forgotten. The hamburgers looked like charcoal briquettes. They were burnt to a crisp. He scooped them up with a spatula, put them into a pan, and turned off the gas. "Brady, go shower and get dressed. We're going out to eat."

"Aw, Dad. I want to swim some more."

"Maybe I can get off work early tomorrow afternoon, too. You can swim then."

"But, Dad—"

"Want a milkshake with your hamburger?"

"Yippee!"

❧

Jeris took a sip of water, then glanced around at the pink, yellow, and green light-tube signs in Jolly Hamburgers. The signs announced the restaurant's specialties. HAMBURGERS.

MILKSHAKES. FRENCH FRIES. "Where's Martin this time, Carrie?"

Carrie's mouth was a grim line across her otherwise pretty face. "Miami again. Fifth time in a row."

Jeris's heart went out to Carrie. She was having a hard time coping with Martin's traveling. "At least his trips are only once a month."

"I know. I should be thankful. One of the women in my Sunday school class is alone three weeks out of four. Her husband travels internationally. But somehow that doesn't help my feelings. Martin's been going to Miami so often lately that I asked him about our moving down there so we wouldn't be apart as much."

"You'd leave me? What would our office do without you?"

"It's not going to happen. His company wants him here."

"Whew. That's a relief." Jeris paused, feeling guilty. "For me, at least." She swallowed hard. "Maybe something'll happen so he won't have to travel anymore."

Carrie nodded.

The waitress came and took their orders, Jeris's first.

Jeris settled back comfortably in the red leather booth as the waitress took Carrie's order. She listened to the lively, upbeat music that appealed to adults and children alike. She liked coming to Jolly Hamburgers. Every now and then she craved a hamburger, and Jolly's had the best in town—*after* homemade ones. Her father used to grill a lot when she was growing up, and he always said the best food in the world was a homemade, home-grilled hamburger with a slice of sweet onion on top. She couldn't agree more.

"Have you thought any more about alpha and beta men, Jeris?"

One.

"Remember that book I was telling you about? About heroes?"

Oh, I remember.

"Miss Jeris!" Brady came rushing up the aisle.

Jeris leaned sideways and gave him a big hug when he reached her. "Hi, Brady. What are you doing here?" She glanced down the long row of booths. Luke was probably still in the lobby, waiting on the hostess to get their menus.

"Miss Jeris, Dad burned our hamburgers. So we had to come and buy one. And he said I could have a milkshake with mine."

"I'll bet that suits you just fine, Little Man." She tapped him on the chin, then glanced down the long row of booths again. She could feel her face growing warm. Luke would be approaching any moment. She remembered what Audra Darling had told her. She felt as vulnerable and shy as a kid on the first day of kindergarten.

Luke walked up from out of nowhere, it seemed. "Hi, Jeris."

A bolt of courage hit her. Audra Darling would call it Holy Spirit illumination. She smiled. "Hi, Luke. Well, fancy meeting you here." She jumped up and gestured at Carrie. "I'd like you to meet my friend Carrie."

Carrie extended her hand and gave Luke a shake and Brady a high-five. "Nice meeting you, Luke, Brady."

"Nice to meet you, Carrie," Luke said.

"Carrie's my office manager. She keeps everything flowing smoothly. She helps with the office work, and sometimes she entertains the kids in the waiting room, and sometimes she—"

"Analyzes people and dispenses advice." Carrie gave Jeris a knowing look.

"She's becoming a pro at that." Jeris smiled at her for a long moment, then turned her attention back to Brady. "So you're getting a hamburger and milkshake tonight, Little Man?"

"Yes, ma'am."

"Are you going to ride the merry-go-round after you eat?"

Brady looked up at Luke, his hands folded under his chin as he jumped from one foot to the other.

They all laughed at his cute antics.

Luke rubbed the top of Brady's head. "I suppose so. How can we resist the call of the carousel?"

Jeris turned to Carrie. "Luke and I rode the merry-go-round on a children's outing a few weeks ago."

"Let me guess. Luke rode the wild stallion seahorse, and you rode the gentle sea cow, the manatee."

"There you go again, analyzing people." She batted her eyelashes, Carrie-style, enthusiasm welling up within her. She liked that feeling. It felt good. "No. I rode a dolphin, and Luke"—she gestured at him with a flourish and a smile—"sat safely on one of those benches on the first tier. Are you going to ride a sea creature this time, Luke? Or sit on the bench again?"

He looked intently into her eyes. "Maybe I won't get on the merry-go-round at all. Maybe I'll stand at the gate and talk with you while Brady rides."

A little tingle surged up her spine. "That sounds. . .like. . ."

"Sounds like fun to me, Miss Jeris," Brady piped up.

She smiled down at Brady as she and Luke made plans, the tingles lingering along her spine. They agreed to meet at the merry-go-round after they finished eating. Her heart was singing.

The hostess came and asked Luke and Brady to follow her. Within moments they'd said good-bye and disappeared from view.

"How's your writing coming along, Carrie?" Jeris asked. "How many more chapters have you written?"

"Only two. Lately I've been studying the craft almost as much as I've been writing."

The waitress set chocolate milkshakes on the table, then left.

"Yum, yum." Carrie took a long sip through her straw, sat back against the booth, and let out a lengthy sigh. "This is almost as good as reading a Christian romance novel."

Jeris sipped her chocolate shake, savoring the flavor.

"They may be pure escapism, but they're fun to read. And they always have a scriptural theme, at least the ones I've read. And they're so satisfying. Throughout the story the hero won't admit he loves the heroine, or she him. He's noble and brave and dashing though she may not realize it at first, but he has a toughness about him that puts her off."

"Let's see." Jeris winked as she wrote on a pretend notebook with a pretend pen. "The patient has an obsession for Christian romance novels—"

"I really don't."

"I know. It's entertainment."

"Exactly. Some people sew or watch TV or go to movies or do crafts or whatever. I read good Christian books."

"I read them, too. They're more uplifting than what's on TV. Some of that stuff is getting raunchy."

"You're telling me. I'll take an inspiring novel any day over TV or movies." Carrie sighed the same long sigh she had earlier. "By the end of the book the hero's so hopelessly in love with the heroine and so captivated by her charms that he asks, 'What do I have to do to make you mine?' The heroine is so in love with him by this point that she says, 'I'm yours, mister.'" She laughed, then grew quiet and let out a low groan. "Oh, boy, do I miss Martin."

Jeris sensed Carrie's pain at their forced separation. "Your real obsession is Martin Denton."

"You couldn't be any more insightful, Dr. Waldron." Carrie gave her a sappy look as she whipped out a picture of Martin and kissed it. "I'm yours, mister."

They burst into laughter as Carrie had done before.

"I'm feeling sort of giddy tonight," Jeris said.

"I'd call it euphoric."

"How so?"

"It's because you just talked to the love of your life."

"The love of my life?" Jeris was enjoying their banter.

Carrie nodded, her head bobbing up and down like the

trinket on a pickup's dashboard. "From everything you've told me about Luke, I think he's a sensational man. He's the *rara avis*. That's Latin for 'rare bird'—or, in my words, 'one in a thousand.'"

Jeris considered this. A warm glow flushed through her.

"I'll tell you something else I think."

"What's that?"

"I've studied this alpha and beta thing so much that I think I can confidently predict that Luke is an alpha male. But my woman's intuition tells me he's got enough beta in him to make an excellent husband."

"A what?" Jeris unrolled her silverware from the napkin. The fork slipped and landed with a *clink* on the floor.

"You heard me. A husband." Carrie paused. "Jeris?"

"Yes?"

"Amor vincit omnia."

"Latin for—?"

"'Love conquers all.'"

❧

Luke draped his arm on the wrought iron fence that separated the onlookers from the riders of the merry-go-round. He glanced at Jeris standing beside him. She was waving at Brady every time he came around. She looked so pretty tonight.

Her outfit showed off her slenderness, and her hair was just the way he liked it. She was wearing her smooth updo, not her ponytail, though that appealed to him, too. Both styles spoke of casualness, and knowing her love for the outdoors, they were perfect for a woman with those interests.

But the prettiest thing about her was her inward beauty. He remembered the verse in Timothy. Or was it Peter?

"Dad, watch me!"

Luke looked over at Brady as he whizzed by on a seal, hunched forward and jiggling the reins as if he were on a live bucking bronco. "Hang on, Brady." He glanced at Jeris and smiled. "I wouldn't want that seal to buck him."

She laughed, her eyes shining as she looked at him.

He stood there enjoying the pleasant sensation passing between them and the lilting sounds of her laughter as if they were floating across a cloud. Her laughter was musical and sounded better than the enchanting tunes coming from the merry-go-round, and it mesmerized him.

For a long moment he let his gaze feast on her—on her striking olive-toned skin, her pleasing features, her captivating smile, the slimness of her form, her animated movements as she waved at Brady.

"What are you thinking about, Luke?"

It's too soon to put my feelings into words.

She waved again as Brady came by. "I enjoy having Brady in my class. He loves to hear the Bible stories when it's story time."

"He says you either act them out or get the kids to do it. He likes that, dressing up in Bible costumes."

She nodded. "We live in a media-saturated world, and that's what we're competing with in the church. I try to make things as lively as I can. I want the Bible to come alive for the kids."

"I, for one, want to thank you for all you're doing for the children at Christ Church."

"Thanks, Luke."

"I intend to help more."

"You do?"

"I've cut back on my long hours."

"Good." She smiled up at him, playfully batting her eyelashes. "Can you chaperone another outing? We're taking the kids on a picnic and boat ride at the parsonage this coming Sunday, right after church."

❧

Luke and Brady walked Jeris to her vehicle in the mall parking lot. They waved good-bye to her as she drove off, then found their car six or seven aisles away.

As they buckled up, Luke thought about Jeris and her love for Brady.

He blinked hard. *Her love for Brady?*

He could see it every time they were together. Her love for his son shone in her eyes and in her actions.

What did that mean for the future? For *their* future? Was this headed into a future that included the three of them? He hoped so.

He remembered Brady's prayer, when he asked God to send him a mommy.

Was Jeris that person? Would she turn out to be the right wife Mr. Granfield had written about? The wife for Luke Moore?

There was only one way to explore this.

Ask her for a date.

೩

After she got home from the mall, Jeris sat on a barstool in her kitchen, reading Wednesday's and Thursday's mail. That happened sometimes, having to read two days' worth of mail. It had been a busy week.

She read awhile, then grew distracted, thinking about the evening she'd spent with Luke and Brady. She and Luke had talked a lot, and not once had she felt shy or awkward around him. On the contrary, it had been wonderful.

R–r–r–i–i–ing.

She picked up her phone and looked at the readout. *Luke.* Was something wrong? Brady? She clicked it on. "Luke?"

"Hi, Jeris."

"Is everything all right?"

"Why do you ask?"

"I was worried. We just saw each other less than thirty minutes ago."

"We did? I thought it was thirty days ago." He laughed.

The tingles hit her spine. Was he saying time went by slowly when he was away from her? She was finding that was true for her.

"Are you sure we were together tonight?" He laughed again.

She laughed along with him.

"Excuse me for being silly, Jeris."

"No excuses needed." *I like what you're saying, Luke.* She got brave. "I like what you're saying, Luke."

"Hmm." He purred like a cat. Loudly.

The sounds coming over the phone thrilled her. A cat purred when it was happy. Or so the theory went. "Luke. . ."

"Jeris. . ."

"Da–a–a–d!"

Jeris could hear Brady hollering in the background.

"Jeris, can you hang on a sec?" Luke asked. "I'll be right back."

"Sure." She waited a couple of minutes.

"Jeris?" he finally said. "You still here?"

"I'm here. Is Brady all right?"

"He's fine. Thanks for waiting. Brady didn't know I was on the phone, and I had to go check on him. He said he had to tell me he loved me one more time—before he fell asleep." His voice choked up. "That little fellow. . .I'm sorry. I didn't mean to get emotional on you."

"It's okay. I'm a good listener."

"I forgot. You're a psychologist."

"Is anything bothering you? Is there anything you want to talk about? Something I could help you sort through or understand better?"

A long pause ensued.

"I'm sorry, Luke. I didn't mean to sound so professional. Forgive me?"

"For what? You saw a person all choked up, and something kicked in for you—empathy, I'd say. That's probably what makes you a good psychologist."

"Thanks, Luke. Are things going well for you and Brady? I mean, I'm sure they are. Every time I'm around you two, I can't get over how well-adapted he seems to. . .to his. . ." Now she was faltering for words.

"To his circumstances? You mean, a child without a mother?"

She cringed. Had she made him feel uncomfortable? She hadn't meant to.

"That's sort of why I called you." He paused. "At least it's along those lines."

"What do you mean?"

"I called to ask if you'd like to go out with me."

Oh, my. She stood up from the barstool quickly, nearly knocking it over, as surprised as an honoree at a birthday party. Actually she was more thrilled than surprised. If that could be so. *I'd love to go out with you, Luke.*

"Do you have plans for this Saturday night? I know it's awfully soon to spring this on you."

Saturday night? She wouldn't be home in time from Tampa. She and Audra Darling were going shopping at the new mall. Maybe she could cancel her plans. She'd rather be with Luke. Her breath came in short, jerky puffs.

"Jeris? Did we get cut off?"

"I'm here."

"I thought we'd go out to eat at one of those fancy places— a nice steakhouse or a seafood restaurant on the water. We could get lobster if you like. We can go anywhere you want to. . . ."

"Jolly's would be fine with me." *As long as it's with you.*

"It would?"

"Yes."

"Well, I have better places in mind than that. And, after we eat, I thought maybe we could go to the concert at the beach—that is, if you'd like to. People spread blankets on the grassy area, and the orchestra plays from the band shell. The Silver Bay Symphony is performing. Some people eat out there. They bring their own picnics. Or they buy their food at the food stands—"

"I—I can't go." *This is painful, Luke. You don't know how painful.*

"You can't?"

"I already made plans with Audra Darling for Saturday. We won't be back in time."

"O–o–h–h."

She remembered what Audra Darling had said about her and Luke, how she thought they were made for each other. She recalled what else she'd said. *"When—and not if—Luke asks you out, be prepared."* She'd been so. . ."euphoric" this evening— what Carrie called it—that she'd been caught off guard by his call. But she could remedy that.

"Well. . ." His voice trailed off.

"I'm free tomorrow night, Luke."

"You are? You don't mind having only one day's notice for a date?"

"Not at all. I'd *love* to go out with you tomorrow night."

"Yippee!" he shouted.

She laughed.

He laughed, too. "That just slipped out."

eighteen

On the way to the restaurant Luke took covert peeks at Jeris. She was beautiful. Her ocean blue eyes sparkled like aquamarines in a necklace. They were noteworthy and so light blue green they looked almost translucent, as if they glittered. Why hadn't he noticed their beauty before?

He glanced at her again. Her hair was in that style he liked so well, and a few pieces floated softly about her temples and in front of her ears. Her hair wasn't blond, and it wasn't brown. It was in between but not streaky with that dyed stuff some women used. It was natural, he was sure, and it was beautiful. Why hadn't he noticed the striking color before?

He smiled, thinking about Miss Ada's booklet. It had some good advice, though it was archaic. But the basic tenets still held true. *The right wife?* In the book, Mr. Granfield said a man needed to look for a woman who was a Christian before he considered anything else. Jeris met that requirement. Then he talked about finding a woman who served the Lord and put Him first in her life. Jeris met that one, too. Then he discussed inward beauty, which Mr. Granfield interpreted as being kind and good and unselfish. Jeris possessed not only inward beauty but also outward beauty—

"We're both quiet this evening," she said.

He nodded. "I was thinking. . . ."

"Me, too."

"You were?" He cast another sideways look at her, and their gazes held for a moment. He forced himself to look back at the road. Was she thinking what he was? About the *M* word? But he chided himself. It was too soon. Though he'd known her a full three months, he reminded himself he needed to go slowly. "What were you thinking about?"

"I—I was thinking how odd it seems not having Brady with us."

"I know. But I'm sure he's enjoying being with Mrs. Nelms. She reads dozens of books to him when she baby-sits." He paused. "I apologize again for this last-minute date."

"I'm glad you didn't wait."

He took a moment to digest that.

"I'm looking forward to this evening." She brushed a strand of hair away from her temple.

Glancing her way, he took note of her hands as she fiddled with her hair and her simple blue top that accentuated her eyes as if it had been a piece of jewelry.

"Where are we going?"

"I was going to ask you for your preference. Steak? Lobster? Whatever. What are your taste buds craving?"

"I have this idea. . . ." Her voice grew quieter with each word she spoke. "I don't know if you'd like to do it—"

"Try me."

"What if we pick up some sandwiches and chips at the deli and go to the band shell?"

"But the concert is tomorrow night."

"I know."

&

With Luke behind her, Jeris made her way to a tall palm tree, its fronds swaying gently in the ocean breeze. A pastel-colored light shone up its trunk. She saw other palm trees nearby. All had pastel-colored lights shining up them. The setting was extraordinary. Her heart beat a little trill inside her chest. "What about here?"

"That looks like a good place." Luke caught up to her and spread a beach towel on the soft grass that fronted the gigantic but empty band shell. "Good thing I started keeping a towel in my trunk. I've taken Brady to the beach a few times on the spur of the moment, and it's come in handy."

"It came in handy this evening, too." She sat down on one end. She could hear the lulling sound of the waves behind the sand dunes that separated the grass they were sitting on from the beach—a symphony in its own right.

He sat down beside her, the grocery bags still in his hands.

The confines of the towel were tight. Glancing down, she noticed only an inch or two of orange and yellow between them, forcing her to keep her shoulders erect. He would have to do the same thing. If she'd been fair-skinned, she'd be blushing at their closeness.

"Our own private picnic."

She let the waves do the talking, their constant ebb and flow echoing the beating of her heart.

"I'm glad you thought of this," he said.

"I didn't know this place would be so. . .so. . ."

"Romantic?" His eyebrows wiggled up and down, and lights danced in his eyes.

She gave a quick nod. "I haven't been to Silver Bay's bandshell before. When I suggested it, I was only thinking *picnics* and *outdoors*."

"Would you have suggested it if you'd known what it was like?" He looked into her eyes, and it was as if their gazes were locked.

"Yes." Her heart beat so hard that she was afraid he'd see her shirt vibrating. But she couldn't draw her gaze away from his. She noticed how the wind was ruffling his dark hair, how his hair seemed to prance about in the gentle breeze. She basked in his nearness. She could smell his masculine cologne and could have felt the smoothness of his jaw if she had reached out and touched it. She wondered what it would be like to kiss him, to feel his lips on hers. . . .

"Goldie!" someone shouted from across the way. "Come here to me. Don't bother those people."

Jeris felt a dog's snout at her back, then at her elbow. "Ooh." She giggled. The dog's nose felt cold to her skin. He touched her elbow again. "Ooh!" she exclaimed. It tickled.

Luke laughed when he saw the dog, a golden retriever. He bared his teeth in fun, and the dog let out a ferocious bark.

" 'Hark, hark, the dogs do bark.' " Jeris giggled. "That's a nursery rhyme."

"Goldie Johnson," a lady's voice snapped. "Quit your nosing around, and come here this instant."

The retriever took off across the grass, as excited as a child running into the waves.

"So much for romantic moments." Luke shrugged his shoulders, but he was grinning from ear to ear, as if what had just happened was hilarious.

They both laughed.

Jeris looked down at the grocery bags he was holding. "Want me to unwrap our sandwiches?"

"Sure." He handed her one of the bags and reached into the other one. "I'll get our soft drinks out." He handed her one. "Want me to pray?"

"Yes."

"Lord, thank You for Your goodness in our lives. Thank You for giving us this evening together in this magnificent place—one created by Your hand. Help us to count for Your kingdom and our lives for Your service. Now bless our food and this glorious time. In Jesus' name. Amen."

"That was a beautiful prayer, Luke."

He smiled and nodded as he held up his sandwich. "Chow down."

She picked up her sandwich and took a bite. His prayer had stirred her. She recalled what Carrie had said about him last night at the mall. She thought he was one in a thousand. The warm glow hit her again, rushing through her with gale forces.

They ate in silence, except for the sound of the waves, then talked awhile, then ate, then talked.

It seemed to Jeris their souls communed as they sat under a

velvety, star-studded sky. An Emily Brontë verse came to her. *"Whatever our souls are made of, his and mine are the same."* She shivered, and it wasn't from the ocean breeze.

≥

I wonder if we would've kissed if the dog hadn't come up?

Luke smiled as he drove home after taking Jeris to her apartment. Though he hadn't planned to kiss her on their first date, he might've done it. It would've just seemed right. And good. And fitting.

He couldn't think of any more adjectives.

All he *could* think of was her. He wanted to be with her every minute and couldn't wait until the next time they were together.

When would that be?

Oh, yes. Day after tomorrow. Sunday. She'd asked him to be a chaperone for the children's outing at the parsonage.

How would he make it all day tomorrow without seeing her?

≥

Jeris sat down on the edge of her bed and picked up her alarm clock. The red digital numbers glowed against the black background—1:30 a.m. She set it for 7:00. She had to get up early for her shopping outing with Audra Darling.

She crawled in and settled under the covers, but she was too exhilarated to sleep. She was as wide awake as if it had been 1:30 in the afternoon instead of in the morning. She let out a satisfied sigh. Throughout their evening together, the romantic sparks had never let up. Oh, it wasn't a physical sensation necessarily. He hadn't even touched her.

She remembered when he'd almost kissed her and probably would have, if the dog hadn't shattered the magical moment. She didn't believe in kissing on a first date. But somehow, with Luke, it would've been all right. And it would've been a light, feathery kiss. She just knew.

Later, when they walked on the beach, he didn't even

hold her hand or put his arm around her shoulders. Yet something indescribable had happened between them. Their souls communed. That's what came to her earlier, and that's what came to her now.

She smiled when she recalled how late it was as they drove home. One a.m. She had thought of the nursery rhyme "Hickory Dickory Dock," the verse about the clock striking one and "the mouse did run." She had quoted it, and they'd laughed together.

Luke apologized profusely for bringing her home so late, telling her he hadn't realized the lateness of the hour, how time had slipped away from him.

She told him time had slipped away from her, too, as the old adage filled her thoughts. *Time flies when you're having fun.*

Only *fun* was too weak a word to describe what had transpired between them tonight.

nineteen

Jeris stood in the fitting room, staring at herself in the three-way mirror. She grasped a handful of lightweight, flowing fabric at thigh level. "You really think I ought to wear a print, Audra Darling? I always wear solids."

"As sure as I'm standing here."

"It's not very businesslike."

"It's perfect. You look like a dream come true, dah-ling."

Jeris glanced down at the outfit Audra Darling had picked out for her.

"You're wearing a fine-gauge knit, aqua-colored shrug—"

"Did you say a 'shroud'?"

"Jeris, you are a mess."

Jeris laughed.

"You crazy thing, you. It's not a *shroud*. It's a *shrug*. A shrug is a short knit jacket. And this one has a matching camisole. And your aqua-and-black knee-length skirt has a ruffled hem that's made of lined georgette."

"It's beautiful."

Audra Darling leaned over and peered at Jeris's calf. "You've got a little leg going on there, girlfriend. That's a nice feature. Anybody ever tell you you have well-shaped legs, Jeris? Like a ballerina's?"

Jeris playfully swatted her away and looked in the mirror again, pleased with how the outfit looked, with how *she* looked.

"Aqua's a great color with your eyes. And the skirt's ruffled hemline brings some femininity to the ensemble."

"Ever thought about being one of those—what are they called—a caller?" Jeris giggled. "At fashion shows—when the models walk down the runway and someone describes what they're wearing?"

"I used to sew my clothes years ago. That's why I know some of these terms. And I watch those makeover shows on TV sometimes. You know, the ones where they select new clothing and hairstyles and makeup?" She clasped her hands together. "I love to see befores and afters. I love those shows."

"You can tell. You've got the lingo *going on*." Jeris giggled again.

Audra Darling ignored her. "And your shoes—you have a heel thing happening. And some nice toe action."

Jeris looked down at her black high heels with their narrow ankle straps. "Good thing I painted my toenails last night."

"How late was it when Luke brought you home?"

"I'll never tell." She was having that euphoric feeling again. "But I painted them before we went out. I'm glad I did. We took off our shoes and went for a walk on the beach."

"Ooh–la–la."

"In the moonlight."

R–r–r–i–i–ing.

"That's mine. I'll get it." Jeris reached for her new metallic-colored satchel with the double shoulder straps and rhinestone detail. Audra Darling had insisted she buy it earlier in another store. She retrieved her cell phone, saw it was Luke, felt her heart do a trill, and clicked it on. "Hi, Luke."

"Hi, Jeris. I—I wanted to say hello."

"Hello to you, too."

"I was wondering—what are you doing today?"

Is that longing in his voice? He's missing me. And I'm missing him. "I'm shopping with Audra Darling."

"Oh, yes. You told me that. I forgot."

"You know what she's like. She's a shopaholic. She never wears out. We went to three stores before lunch, and she tells me we have four more places to go to before we can call it quits for the day."

"Well, I wouldn't want to keep you then."

Keep me! Keep me!

"I guess I'll let you go."

Don't ever let me go!

"All Brady's talked about is the children's outing. He can't wait to see you tomorrow."

The children's picnic and boat ride. . .and being with Luke.

"And, Jeris? Neither can I."

❧

Luke clicked Solitaire off his laptop in his home office and glanced at the phone. He'd like to call Jeris again. He wanted to talk to her, to hear her voice. But he'd called her less than an hour ago, and he didn't want to be a bother.

He whirled around in his roller chair and came to a stop facing the large palladian window overlooking his front lawn. Maybe he should go work in the yard. Though his yard guy mowed the grass and edged the concrete every week, some of his shrubs needed a deep pruning. No, he'd call the guy and hire him to do it.

Maybe he should take a swim in the pool. No, it wasn't any fun without Brady, who was attending a birthday party and wouldn't be home for hours.

Maybe he should do some of the work he'd brought home from the office. No, he couldn't focus—on anything. All he could think about was Jeris.

All day he'd pined for her. What an interesting way to put it. Maybe he'd seen the word in the old-fashioned booklet. Archaic, he knew. But it spoke of what he felt. He was acting like a lovesick teenager having his first brush with love. But it couldn't be helped. She did that to him.

He'd prayed long and hard and sought God for a mate. He now felt Jeris was the one for him. What was his next step? It was too soon to reveal his feelings to her. He might scare her away. And, besides, he respected her too much to do that. They needed time to be together, to find out things about each other and grow to care for each other slowly. But he already cared for her. Still, she needed time for that to happen to her. He was sure it would. He was confident God would work out everything between them. But he could use some practical tips.

What would Mr. Granfield say? In short order he had the booklet in his hands and opened it to the next chapter: "How to Woo Her." He smiled. " 'Woo'? That's an old-fashioned word." Though he knew what it meant, he wanted to see the exact phrasing. He pulled his dictionary off the shelf. " 'Woo: to court a woman.' " He chuckled as he flipped the pages to the old-fashioned word *court*.

" 'Court: to engage in activity leading to mating.' Oops." He searched through the entry for a more appropriate definition. " 'To seek to win a pledge of marriage.' " He threw his arm in the air in a victory signal. "Yes!"

> "Spend as much time as you can with your girl. Seek ways to be with her. There are all sorts of social and church functions you can attend together. Converse with her freely. Come to know, trust, and love her, just as she will come to know, trust, and love you. This is a process and will take some time. Don't rush it. Put the Lord first in your relationship. At times pray together.
>
> Remember that the Lord wants to help you in all ways as you pursue courtship—the most important area of your life after salvation. Just as God guided Abraham's trusted servant to find a bride for his son Isaac, so He will guide you. God inclined the lovely maiden Rebekah to accept the proposal to become Isaac's bride, and the Bible says when they came together Isaac loved her. It also says she comforted him. One definition of *comfort* is 'a satisfying or enjoyable experience.' "

Oh, yes!

"Lad, be friendly. Be courteous. Be gentlemanly."

Of course.

"Though morality is at an all-time low in today's world, the Christian lad and girl will not take liberties with their bodies while dating. Even though God created a lad and girl with innate physical desires for each other, they must not indulge in illicit love. Strive with all your hearts to come to each other in marriage clean and pure. When you say 'I do,' you may enjoy each other's caresses in ecstasy all the days of your lives."

Hallelujah!

"Now for some practical matters. Use plenty of soap and water when preparing yourself to be with your girl. Avoid B.O. like the Grim Reaper."

Oh, brother!

"Trim your nails. Comb your hair. Shine your shoes. Wear some good-smelling toilet water."

Luke started laughing.

"And always wear jaunty neckties."

Still laughing, he tossed the booklet in the air.

❧

Jeris finished her salad, then drank the last of her sweet iced tea. They'd stopped in a restaurant on their way home after shopping all day. It was now dark, and she was bone tired.

"I guess it's time to call it a day." Audra Darling discreetly applied pink lipstick as she looked into a miniature mirror clipped to a tube. Then she snapped it shut and dropped it into her turquoise crocheted shoulder bag that matched her turquoise crocheted espadrilles.

"I don't think I'll ever look at clothes and shoes and purses in quite the same way after today." Jeris took out her own miniature mirror clipped to her lipstick tube—identical to Audra Darling's and purchased during today's shopping. She glanced at the bottom of the tube. "Transcendent Sunrise." She applied it quickly, then dropped it back into her purse.

After you eat, touch up your lipstick fast, Audra Darling had said. *People will hardly notice what you're doing.*

"I like your new makeup," Audra Darling said. "It looks good on you."

Jeris touched her cheek. Audra Darling had taken her to a makeup counter in a fine department store, and the clerk had given her a makeover. "I kept telling her to go easy, and she did, from what I can tell. What differences do you see between the old me and the new me?"

"That light touch of shadow is nice. It enhances your eye color even more. And the blush brings out your cheekbones. I never noticed how high they are. And the mascara gives the perfect upsweep to your eyelashes. And the lipstick is the cherry on top of the sundae."

"Thanks for today, Audra Darling. How can I ever repay you?"

"Just wear those pretty clothes."

Jeris nodded, thinking about her new outfits and shoes and two purses.

"You're now the proud owner of"—Audra Darling held out her hand, palm side up. She grasped her pinkie finger, her silver charm bracelet jangling—"a black cropped mandarin-collar jacket, rose-and-black lace cami, and rose crinkle skirt with stretch lace trim." She grasped her ring finger. "And a vanilla long-sleeved V-necked blouse, gold jacquard vest, and brown dress gauchos." She took hold of her middle finger. "And a—"

"All right, already. Just condense it to 'Jeris Waldron is now the proud owner of eight colorful new *feminine* outfits.'"

Audra Darling reached over the table and flicked the ends of Jeris's hair where they hit her shoulder. "And she's sporting a new hairstyle, too."

Jeris touched her sleek, feather-cut, blow-dried hairdo. "I love it. But it'll be back in its twist or ponytail soon, I can tell you that."

"That's okay. I just wanted you to see what you looked like with another style. This'll give you more choices. You know which outfit I like best of all the ones you bought today?"

Jeris thought for a moment. "Let me see if I have the gift of description like you do. Is it my black sleeveless square-neck dinner dress with the flounced knee-length hemline?"

"Guess again."

"My, you're putting me to work. Is it my brown cotton-spandex fitted jacket with the coordinating brown-and-aqua print skirt with the"—she stared out the window, thinking—"what kind of pleats?"

"It's called a yoke skirt with inverted pleats."

"A yoke skirt with inverted pleats." She swiped at her forehead dramatically. "I passed, even if I didn't get one hundred." She smiled.

"That outfit's gorgeous. But my favorite of all the clothes you bought is your white sleeveless, fitted, V-necked Battenburg-lace-trimmed dress—"

"With the princess seams."

Audra Darling nodded and smiled. "You're getting good at this."

"I have a good teacher."

"Princess seams emphasize all the right places. You're going to be a knockout in it, what with your olive skin and aqua eyes. I can't wait for Luke to see you in it."

"You don't have to wait too long. I'm wearing it to church tomorrow." The tingles surged up her spine.

twenty

"Finish your cereal, Little Man." Luke pushed his empty bowl aside, then reached for his Bible on the counter behind them. "It'll soon be time to go to church." He found the chapter, looked down, and began reading his portion for the day.

"Is this the day we get to go on the boat ride?"

"That's right," Luke said distractedly, his eyes on the page before him. "Miss Jeris is having a picnic at the Hugheses' for your class."

"I get to see Miss Jeris. Yippee!"

Luke looked up, focusing on the framed print behind Brady's head. But he wasn't seeing the Italian countryside with its earthy tones of rust and brown and tan that he'd looked at a hundred times and more. He was seeing Jeris. Jeris with her class. Jeris with Brady. Jeris with *him*.

"She's so much fun, Dad." If Brady had been standing, he would've been jumping. As it was, he was still jumping—sitting down, his upper body jiggling in movement. "I get to see her today. I get to see her today. I get to see her today."

I get to see her today. I get to see her today. I get to see her today.

Brady bolted out of his chair. "I'm through eating." He swiped at his mouth with a napkin.

"Put your cereal bowl in the sink and go brush your teeth. Then put on your clothes and socks and shoes. I laid them out in your room. If you get finished with that and have time, you can play a video game."

"Yes, Dad."

In seconds Luke was alone in the kitchen, Brady's high-pitched chirps boomeranging down the hall.

He straightened his tie—jaunty? He smiled as he continued

reading the Bible. But he couldn't concentrate.

Mr. Granfield again? Why not? He had a little time before they needed to leave for church. And he was in the mood for some—entertainment?

He scooped up *How to Choose the Right Wife. . .for Christian Lads* and opened it.

"How Can You Tell If It's the Real McCoy?" He could skip that chapter. He already knew the answer. Oh, well.

> "How do you decide if this is the Real McCoy? Is this true love or puppy love? Will the feelings you are having last throughout eternity or until the next pretty girl comes along? You must think about the following questions. Did you put this matter in God's hands? Did you diligently seek Him for your mate? Is she a Christian? Does she have sweetness of spirit? Does she possess inner beauty? Do the two of you have common interests? Does she have high moral standards? What are your answers thus far?"

A definite yes on each one.

> "Let's hope your answers are in the affirmative."

Oh, yes.

> "Through seeking the Lord, I assure you, you will be able to determine if it's true love. You will be able to decide if you have found your sweetheart. Here are some more indications. Is this girl constantly in your thoughts?"

Yes!

> "Do the minutes turn into hours when you're away from her?"

Yes!

"When you think of the future, does it include her?"

Oh, yes!

"Can you see her standing in welcome at the door of your future home-with-the-picket-fence, wearing an apron and holding a spoon?"

"Nosirreebob," he belted out, Miss Ada-style, as he tossed the booklet into the air, laughing so hard that tears came to his eyes.

⁂

Jeris walked into Audra Darling's kitchen. The children's party would start when everyone arrived. She and Audra Darling had told the parents to have the children there by one o'clock and invited them to stay for the afternoon if they'd like. The parents were bringing the fried chicken, Jeris had bought the potato salad at a deli, Audra Darling had made her special-recipe baked beans, and Luke had volunteered to purchase soft drinks.

Standing at the kitchen counter, Audra Darling was making peanut butter and jelly sandwiches, stacks of them, for the children who wanted them.

"Can I help?" Without waiting for an answer, Jeris washed her hands, picked up a knife, and cut the sandwiches in two, then placed them on a large platter.

"Shouldn't you change clothes? That dress would look awful with grape jelly down the front."

"I plan to." Jeris glanced down at her white sleeveless, V-necked Battenburg-lace-trimmed dress. "I wouldn't mess this up for the world. It was too much fun wearing it. I feel like a princess."

"You look like one, too. But are you sure it's the dress

making you feel that way?" Audra Darling elbowed her and winked.

Luke strode into the kitchen, carrying a big cooler.

"Hi, Luke." Audra Darling tipped her head in Luke's direction, then elbowed Jeris for the second time.

Jeris playfully elbowed her back as she thought about the praying she'd done lately. She'd been thanking God for Luke.

"Hi, Audra, Jeris," he said.

"Hi." Jeris felt little tingles hit her spine. Every time Luke came near, she felt that way. She glanced down at her dress again. She hadn't seen him at church this morning. She wondered what he thought about her new clothing and hairstyle. What would he say?

"Where do you want me to put this, Audra?" He gestured at the cooler. "It's full of soft drinks. I have another one in the car."

Audra Darling pointed to the window with a peanut butter-laden knife. "Out there. On the lanai. That's where we're going to eat."

"Okay." He turned and left the room.

"I shouldn't have poked you when Luke came in," Audra Darling whispered. "That was silly. I'll try not to do it again. I'll try to act my age." She winked. "It's just that I'm thrilled with what's happening between you two. But I promise to stand back and let the Lord have His way."

"Thanks. Audra Darling?"

"Hmm?"

"I need to thank you for your part in getting us together."

Audra Darling pointed upward.

Jeris nodded, knowing she was giving total credit to the Lord.

In a few minutes Luke came back inside. "I have the coolers situated. What else needs to be done?" He walked over to them and stood there.

Jeris's heart beat its familiar little trill.

"Luke?" Audra Darling put her knife down, wiped the

peanut butter off her hands, and leaned against the counter.

"Yes?"

"You asked what you can do. You can give your opinion. What do you think about Jeris's new look? That beautiful dress she's wearing? And the way she's fixing her hair now? And the makeup?"

Jeris stopped arranging the sandwiches on the platter, feeling her face flush. She sent Audra Darling a you-said-you-wouldn't-do-this glance.

Audra Darling let out a little gasp and shot Jeris an I-forgot-I'm-sorry look. She waved in the air. "Forget what I said, Luke. There's so much to do right now, with the kids coming and all."

"I don't mind giving you my opinion." He did a quick sweep of Jeris, from head to foot. His gaze came to rest on her hair. "I like it." He moved his hand as if to reach up and touch her hair but dropped it back to his side.

Oh, Luke.

He focused on her face, and their gazes locked. Again he had the same hand movement, as if he wanted to reach out and touch her cheek.

Time seemed to stand still for her.

He glanced down at her dress, then looked into her eyes again, his gaze speaking volumes. "Feminine. Nice."

Jeris smiled. The look he gave her warmed her all the way to her toes.

He took another quick scan of her. " 'That fawn-skinned-dappled hair of hers, and the blue eye dear and dewy, and that infantine fresh air of hers. . . .' "

Your voice sounds like the rich, low tones of a mourning dove.

"That's a Robert Browning poem." He took a step closer to her. "Your new look is pretty. But nothing compares with your *inner* beauty."

"Da–a–a–d! Audra Darling! Miss Jeris! They're here. Everyone's getting out of their cars."

Jeris heard Brady, but she couldn't focus on what he'd said. The tenderness flowing between her and Luke was all-consuming.

&

"Will you ride with me in the boat I'm driving, Jeris?" Luke stood on the dock, fastening his bright orange life vest.

"I'd love to." Jeris felt as if she were walking on air instead of weathered boards.

The parents were helping the children put on their life vests, and the adults who'd been chosen to ride in the two boats were vesting up, as well.

Within minutes the boats were filled, and the motors were idling. Though the children were chattering, they were calm and still.

"I guess we pounded safety issues into them so much that they're paying attention to us." She gestured to the kids. "They aren't horsing around like the usual—Mexican jumping beans." She turned around and rubbed the top of Brady's head where he sat on a low seat.

Luke nodded from the driver's seat, his hand on the steering wheel. "They'll remember this day for a long time."

She drew in a breath of salty air mingled with the slight mildewed smell of her life vest that wasn't entirely unpleasant. It stirred memories of boating trips with her parents when she was growing up.

Pastor Hughes, sitting in the driver's seat of the second boat, revved his motor, then brought it back down to idle level. He explained to the children what they would be seeing on the boat ride, his voice carrying across the water as if he were using the pulpit microphone. He named the flora and fauna of the area, then described the marine life. "You might see some roseate spoonbills today and wood storks and painted buntings and sea turtles." He named a few other animals and water creatures. "We may even see some manatees today. Audra Darling and I spotted one last week."

The children let out oohs and ahs.

"Manatees are grayish brown marine mammals in varying lengths up to thirteen feet. They have two small pectoral flippers on their upper bodies which are used for steering and for bringing food to their mouths. They swim by moving their large paddlelike tails in up-and-down motions. Because they're mammals, they have to breathe air—"

"Like humans?" one boy piped up.

"Yes, just like us. Manatees have been known to stay underwater for as long as twenty minutes, but the average interval between breaths is two to three minutes. Sometimes you'll see them bodysurfing in groups. They also play follow-the-leader—"

"Just like us," a little girl said.

Pastor Hughes nodded. "Sometimes they synchronize their activities including breathing, diving, and changing directions. Or you might see a mother and her newborn calf."

The children oohed and ahhed again.

"I'd sure like to see a manatee today." Jeris peered down at the pewter-colored water, then across to the far shore. "I haven't seen one in a long time."

"That would be nice," Luke said.

Pastor Hughes gave a few instructions to Luke, then headed out. Luke followed closely behind him in the wake. The two boats rode along at a steady clip. At intervals Pastor Hughes gave hand signals to Luke, and Luke followed his lead, slowing at times for the children to see certain plants and animals near the shore, then speeding across the water at other times.

Jeris enjoyed watching the children and their expressions of wonderment and glee. She was grateful Audra Darling had suggested this outing. It was good for the kids, and it was good for their parents. Perhaps they'd gain some new church members from it. She hoped so.

After they'd been on the water an hour and a half, Pastor Hughes headed toward the house and waved for Luke to do the same. In minutes both boats reached the dock.

Jeris helped the adults get each child safely out of the boats. She and Luke were the last to walk up the dock to the house. "I think the kids really enjoyed the outing," she said.

He nodded. "It was kind of Pastor Hughes and Audra to host it."

She smiled. "They love entertaining guests out here. It's second nature to them. Who do you think enjoyed it the most? Them or the kids?"

"Me." He shot her a quirky grin.

❧

Luke, Brady, Jeris, Audra, and Pastor Hughes sat at the patio tables on the lanai, chatting and enjoying each other's company in the late afternoon sunshine.

"I'm sleepy, Dad," Brady said.

"Why don't you stretch out on a lounge chair?" Jeris asked.

Brady nodded as he stood up and walked over to the chair.

She followed him and made him comfortable by propping a folded beach towel under his head for a pillow. In moments he was fast asleep. She caressed his cheek, then made her way back to her chair and sat down.

Luke couldn't help thinking how motherly Jeris was to Brady. She was attentive and loving to him. It warmed his heart to see it. "Thanks, Jeris."

She smiled at him.

An hour flew by as the four of them chatted in animated conversation about many subjects, including the children's church class, the church, Luke's work, Jeris's practice, Brady, and other interests they shared.

Luke looked across the water and saw the sun slip a notch lower in the pale blue-gray sky. "I'd sure like to watch the sun set on the water. It must be awesome out here. It's not something I see very often since I don't live on a body of water as you do." He glanced at his watch. "But it's time to go."

"Don't leave yet," Audra Darling said. "Stay and watch it

with us. Andrew and I watch sunsets every chance we get."

"They're breathtaking out here." Pastor Hughes took a sip of his lemonade. "It's like nothing you've ever seen."

"I'm sure it's great." Luke motioned with his hand. "A sunset over the water."

Audra Darling nodded. "Out here it's as if you're seeing two sunsets instead of one. I mean, I've seen sunsets all my life over water. But I've never seen anything quite like this. This water"—she pointed to the river—"becomes a mirror. You won't believe it until you see it."

"Wow." Jeris looked toward the horizon.

"Okay, you've convinced us, Audra," Luke said. "We'd like to see it, wouldn't we, Jeris? Pastor Hughes and Audra's Double Sunset Over Trout River."

"Oh, yes," Jeris said.

"And Little Man?" Luke glanced at Brady who had just sat up on the lounge chair.

Brady rubbed his eyes. "See what, Dad?"

"A double sunset."

"Can I have a root beer first?"

❧

Jeris stood on the high banks of the water, marveling at God's handiwork in front of her. Oak trees with sprawling limbs stood like sentinels on guard to her right and left. Sharp, pointy palmettos dotted the ground that sloped toward the river.

Surely an artist had painted the sky with masterful, giant strokes. In the late afternoon light it had bands of color, a pale blue gray chasing a swath of yellow chasing a neon orange, all streaked horizontally with black ribbons of clouds interlaced throughout. Where the sky met the river stood a bank of trees in varying heights until they tapered off into the water. Below the waterline to her amazement she saw a second sky as Audra Darling had said, two skies if that could be so, right before her eyes.

"It's like a double exposure, isn't it?" Luke said.

Jeris whirled around. "I didn't know you were standing there." She smiled at him. "It's spectacular."

"Yes, it is." He took a step closer to her, so close they could've held hands. His glance scanned her face, from her eyes to her lips, then back to her eyes. "Spectacular," he said in a throaty whisper.

Her heart beat like a drum. A flood of adjectives hit her. *Kind. Good. Gentlemanly. Tender.*

"Let's go sit in the swings on the bank and watch." Audra Darling stepped off the lanai and into the soft grass. "It's a perfect spot to see our double sunset."

"The perfect spot. . ." She hated to leave the place where she and Luke were standing and didn't want to break the sweetness between them. But she nodded and followed Audra Darling across the grass.

Brady caught up to her and locked hands. "Miss Jeris, is the sun going to drop into the water two times?"

She laughed. "No. Only once. But it'll be reflected in the water below. Sort of like when you look in a mirror." As they walked along, she peered down at the cute little boy with the unruly blond hair and freckles. A love so thick she could almost slice it seemed to flow from her heart to his. *A mother's love?* A picture appeared before her eyes of a giant red heart overshadowing her, then melting into her skin in shades of scarlet and fuchsia and pink until her flesh was its natural olive tone again. So this was what a mother's love felt like, to be immersed in *agape*.

Luke and Pastor Hughes followed behind Jeris, Brady, and Audra Darling as they made their way toward the two covered swings under a mammoth oak.

Audra Darling pointed to the first swing. "Jeris, why don't you and Luke sit there?" She didn't wait for an answer. "Brady, come with Pastor Hughes and me. We'll sit in the other one."

Jeris sat down in the swing, and Luke took his place beside

her. Across the way, maybe five yards from them, Audra Darling, Pastor Hughes, and Brady settled in the other swing.

Luke pushed the ground with his foot, and the swing glided into the air in a gentle sway.

Jeris enjoyed the swing's movement. But she enjoyed Luke's nearness more. With a wide expanse of the sky, the tree-dotted horizon and the second sunset reflected in the water; with Luke sitting closely beside her and pleasant thoughts of their future swirling in her head, she thought surely she'd died and gone to heaven. She could sit there forever in this place of beauty, with him close beside her.

"Look." Luke pointed skyward.

The sight Jeris saw took her breath away—what every sunset did to her. The sun dropped faster and faster toward the water in its wide band of orange, the pale blue gray becoming darker with each passing moment. And then it seemed to drop into the water.

No one said anything for some time.

"Look." Pastor Hughes stood. "See that dark circle in the water? I think it's a manatee."

"A manatee?" Brady exclaimed.

Pastor Hughes moved quickly toward the dock. "I'm turning on the hose. If it's a manatee, it'll come to the fresh water."

"Manatees drink from the hose, Dad? Like I do sometimes? When we're out by the pool?"

Audra Darling stood. "Everyone, follow me. I think we're about to see a manatee."

They followed Audra Darling down to the floating dock below.

Jeris walked over to the garden hose on the edge of the dock, a stream of water shooting from its nozzle into the river. To her amazement a dark object swam toward it.

"It's a manatee all right." Pastor Hughes peered into the water.

"A manatee?" Brady said. "Where?"

Jeris took a step toward Brady and put her arm around his shoulders. She pointed downward, toward the dark object in the water. "There. Keep watching."

The manatee surfaced directly under the stream of water flowing from the garden hose. It rolled over on its back, belly up, and opened its mouth, and the water cascaded down its throat.

Jeris was in awe. The manatee wasn't two feet from them. She spotted something beside it. A baby manatee. "Look!" She couldn't help being as excited as Brady always was. "This manatee is a mama. There's her baby."

"Where's a baby, Miss Jeris?" Brady asked.

Jeris pointed to the manatee's side. A smaller version of the manatee hovered close beside her.

"Right there." Luke pointed, too.

"Can you believe it?" Pastor Hughes said. "That calf isn't two weeks old, I'd venture to say."

"Then it's a newborn." Audra Darling came close to the edge. "Oh, how cute." She hummed a few bars of "Rock-a-Bye, Baby." "Brady, that's Mama Manatee and Baby Manatee."

He smiled and looked up at Jeris. "Isn't it cute, Miss Jeris? Her baby? It looks so happy beside its mom."

Jeris's eyes misted over. A manatee and a calf swimming in the water. A woman and a boy standing on the dock. Her heart was so full that she was too overcome to speak.

"Are you okay?" Luke looked into her eyes.

"I'm feeling—spectacular, Luke." She smiled up at him, so happy she could burst.

I'm feeling the same way, his look seemed to say.

The calf submerged, then resurfaced over and over again, but it stayed within a foot of its mother's side.

The adult manatee twirled in the water, then took her same position, lying on her back and drinking the fresh water, gulping it down in huge swallows. After awhile she closed her teeth but kept her lips open so the water rushed over her teeth. Then, of all things, she rubbed her flippers across her teeth.

"Look, Brady!" Audra Darling exclaimed. "Mama Manatee's brushing her teeth."

"She is?"

"Just like you do after you eat," Luke said.

Brady giggled. "Does she have Fred Flintstone toothpaste like me?"

They all laughed.

"What a show." Pastor Hughes shook his head. "Nobody would believe this unless they saw it with their own eyes. A manatee brushing her teeth." He smiled. "I'm glad I have witnesses," he said playfully.

For close to twenty minutes the manatee and her calf stayed at the dock, drinking the fresh water. Finally they swam away.

The five of them stood on the dock watching, even after they couldn't see the manatees any longer, after the sky darkened and the automatic dusk lights came on.

"Thank You, Lord," Pastor Hughes said in the semidarkness, "for allowing us to experience this special time with two of Your remarkable creatures."

Thank You, Lord, Jeris said in her heart, *for allowing me to experience this special time with two of your remarkable creatures, Luke and Brady.*

੨ঌ

Luke walked behind Jeris up the dock toward the parsonage, the dusk lights letting off a dim glow in the darkness. Brady had already gone inside with Pastor Hughes and Audra. Nature had called. It did that a lot with his son. He smiled thinking about it.

He stopped and pointed upward. "Look, Jeris." He leaned against the railing. "I think I see the North Star."

Jeris stopped, too, and looked up. "You're right." She drew in a breath of night air perfumed with a nearby gardenia bush.

"It's in the right position."

A fish jumped out of the water.

Luke looked over the rail into the water that was now as black as midnight. "You got your wish today."

"What's that?"

"You said you wanted to see a manatee."

"Wasn't that something?"

"I don't think I'll ever forget it." Luke recalled how Jeris had teared up when she saw the manatee and her calf together. It was a touching moment that would be branded in his memory forever. Somehow the manatees made him think of her and Brady.

"I won't ever forget it either." Her words were a whisper.

"I can't get over that manatee making motions like she was brushing her teeth."

Jeris laughed.

He laughed, too, remembering the sight, the manatee on her back with her big belly up, her flippers furiously flapping at her teeth.

"You got your wish today, too, Luke."

"I did?"

"Remember? You said you wanted to see a sunset out here."

"And, as Pastor Hughes said, it was breathtaking."

"*They* were breathtaking." She shook her head. "Two sunsets, one mirrored in the water below it."

He turned in the direction of the sunset. *And I know where I want to propose. When the time comes, I want to ask you to marry me right here, Jeris. When the time comes.*

twenty-one

Just as Miss Ada's booklet advised, Luke spent as much time as possible with Jeris over the next few months. They found out nearly everything there was to know about each other. He met her family. She met his. His love for her grew and blossomed and flourished.

He often felt like a runner waiting for the signal as he anticipated the day he would propose, but he wisely bided his time.

❧

Jeris fell in love with Luke slowly. That was the one thing she'd asked the Lord for, if Luke turned out to be the one for her, that she would fall in love with him in a gradual way, not fast like her other love experience had been.

God had let that happen, and now she knew with a surety that Luke was God's choice for her.

They had recently told each other they loved one another. It was the same night they kissed for the first time.

Like a movie, the romantic scene played out in her mind. . . .

❧

"You're tailor-made for me, Jeris," Luke had told her as they sat on a park bench under a starlit sky, walkers and joggers occasionally passing by.

"Tailor-made?" she asked, amused.

"I've been reading an archaic booklet Miss Ada loaned me from the library. The author says the girl God has for a Christian lad will be tailor-made for him."

"Lad?" She giggled.

"It's a hoot. The author says it doesn't matter if the woman has rose-petal lips."

She playfully pursed her lips at him. "Do I have rose-petal lips, Luke?"

He ignored her. "Or cute dimples—"

"Do I have cute dimples?" She poked her fingers in her cheeks.

"Or curly hair."

She patted her head. "Mine's as straight as a board."

"The author says if the girl doesn't have all that, she'll still be the *darlingest* thing in the world."

They laughed as he told her more about the booklet that had kept him intrigued at times, in stitches at others.

Then he told her he loved her, and she told him the same thing, and he called her *my darling* for the first time.

Afterward he took her in his arms and kissed her for the first time.

The only way she could describe it was bliss, pure and simple.

☙

Jeris dressed for her date with Luke, her heart singing as it did every time she went out with him. He'd told her to dress casual. And cool. They would be outdoors, he'd said. She chose a white cotton tiered skirt, a red sleeveless top, and low-heeled white sandals. Luke also told her Brady would be with them tonight. For many of their dates in the past months Mrs. Nelms had baby-sat, though Jeris told him to bring Brady along anytime. And she meant it. She loved Brady almost as much as she loved Luke.

She stood before the mirror, basking in loving thoughts of Luke, and pulled her hair back in the style he liked best, the French twist with the tendrils at her temples.

She heard the doorbell ring, walked to the front door, and opened it. "Luke." She beamed at him.

He stepped inside and hugged her. "You look beautiful, my darling, as always."

She loved the endearing term he frequently called her.

"Thank you. You look good also." He was wearing light khaki pants and a gold shirt that accentuated his brown eyes.

He drew in a deep breath. "You smell nice, as always."

She leaned in close and took in a whiff of his shower-fresh, cologne-splashed skin, enjoying this brief bit of closeness.

"We need to be going. We don't want to be late."

"No." What she really wanted to do was be cocooned in his arms forever. Instead she walked across the room and picked up her purse. "You said. . .Brady was. . .coming?" Their close encounter had left her breathless. She cleared her throat. "Where is he?"

"You'll see."

They stepped out into the early evening sunshine, and she pulled the door shut behind them. Why was he being so mysterious?

In minutes they were in his car, headed for who knew where.

"Where are we going?" She was curious.

"You'll see soon enough."

She nodded. He was being mysterious again. But, as he said, she would soon see. For some dates they'd gone to dinner. Or to concerts or church events. Or social engagements related to Luke's work and picnics at the beach—lots of those. Or swimming, boating, and bicycling. He'd even rented a motorcycle once, and they drove over to the east coast of Florida for the day.

Tonight he had only told her they would be outdoors. That suited her fine. She loved the outdoors. She'd always been a jeans-and-T-shirt-type woman like her mother until she'd become a psychologist. It was then that she started wearing the knit suits, the ones Audra Darling finally told her she detested. She'd worn them to look professional. Now, though, she wore the beautiful clothes Audra Darling had helped her select. She loved them and felt feminine in them, though Luke often said he liked her in casual clothes, too. He said they represented who she was, her active self, the woman he'd fallen in love with. Her breathlessness was back, and she was taking in short, jerky breaths.

"You must be doing some deep thinking." He glanced over at her as he made a right turn off the highway.

"I. . .uh." She figured out where they were headed. "This looks like we're going to the Hugheses'?"

"We are."

She nodded. This would be an evening spent with dear friends. Though it wouldn't be as romantic as she'd first envisioned, it would be a fun evening. "Then why didn't you tell me? Why were you so mysterious?"

"You'll see soon enough."

She playfully tapped him on the forearm and laughed. But she grew quiet immediately. Just the mere touch to his arm sent electric sparks flying up and down her spine. It was a sensation she enjoyed. He told her he'd experienced the same thing. They'd noticed it the first time they kissed, when he held her in his arms on the park bench. After that, they both said no more kissing or holding each other except for brief hugs, and she knew in her heart that they were reserving those things for marriage. Just thinking about it made her breathe even more jerkily.

He made several turns and ended up on the road where the Hugheses lived. He pulled into their driveway and stopped the car, then came around and helped her out.

She could smell something grilling. Steaks? Instead of going to the front door, Luke led her around the side of the house to the backyard.

"Hi, Jeris." Pastor Hughes stood at the grill with a long fork in his hand. Soft, romantic music wafted from a stereo on the lanai.

"Hi, Pastor Hughes. How are you?"

"Miss Jeris!" Brady came bounding toward her and grabbed her at waist level.

"How's my Little Man?" She leaned down and kissed him on the cheek. "I love you."

"I love you, too." He pulled away from her, ran to a horseshoe stob a short distance away, and threw a horseshoe toward it. "Watch me."

It was then she saw it on the banks of the water. An elaborately set table for two surrounded by lighted tiki lamps on tall poles.

"Pastor Hughes and Audra and Brady are eating inside. We're eating out here."

"Oh."

"I thought it would be nice to enjoy a special sunset alone."

⁂

They ate a leisurely dinner with a backdrop of the soft, romantic music. As the sun started setting, the song "I'll Always Love You" came on the player. Luke stood up, walked around the table to her chair, and held out his hand.

She put her hand in his and stood up, though she wondered where they were heading.

He pulled her into a tight embrace.

"This isn't a brief hug," she murmured. She thought her heart would burst from happiness. She felt so good, so safe, so secure in his arms, so in love, so head over heels, so. . .she couldn't think of any more so's.

He pulled her chin up and looked intently into her eyes. Then his face came toward hers, and he kissed her.

"Luke?" she asked, but it came out slurred because of the pressure of his lips on hers. She drew back. "Are we supposed to be doing this?" She was half smiling, wondering what he would say.

"I know. Our NBC policy."

She couldn't help laughing, even in this romantic moment.

He tipped his head toward the windows overlooking the Hugheses' kitchen table. "Look."

Jeris gazed at the windows and saw Audra Darling, Pastor

Hughes, and Brady staring out. She laughed. "What—?"

"This kiss is approved. They're our chaperones for tonight."

She felt the tingles start at the base of her spine and work their way up. When they hit her neck, they started back down and traveled all the way to her ankles.

"This kiss is approved, too." His lips came toward hers.

She giggled, then returned his kiss. She grew dizzy, but it was a good kind of dizzy.

At last he drew away from her. "We can't do that anymore."

She nodded. "I agree."

"Until our wedding."

She nodded again, relishing his closeness. She stopped. He said *wedding*. "Luke?"

He dropped to his knees in front of her.

She drew in a stiff intake of air, then reached for the edge of the table to steady herself.

The back French doors flew open.

From her peripheral vision she saw Brady bounding outside.

Brady ran up to them and plopped in Luke's chair. But he didn't say a word.

She held on to the table tighter. Unusual, she thought, for Brady to be so quiet.

"My darling Jeris." Still on his knees, Luke clasped his hands in front of his chest. "Will you take. . .us"—he pointed to Brady and then to himself—"to have and to hold, from this day forward? For better or worse? For richer or poorer? In sickness and in health? Until death do us part?"

Brady hurled himself out of his chair, knocking it over.

She reached over and righted it.

Brady jumped on one foot, then the other. "Miss Jeris, will you marry us? Please?"

Her heart almost melted, like ice on a hot summer's day.

"Jeris? Will you. . .have us?" Luke gave her a pleading look, his hands still clasped together.

"Oh, yes." She looked long and hard at him, then over at Brady, sending out messages of love. She stared down at Luke again. "A thousand times, yes."

Luke stood, brushing the dirt off his trousers.

Jeris grabbed him in a bear hug. "Hugs are allowed, remember?"

"And so is one more kiss." He winked at her, then tipped his head toward the windows again. "They told me up to three."

She giggled.

He kissed her. But this time it was light and gentle. "Oh, Jeris. . ."

Her heart was pounding. And so was his. She could feel it in their closeness.

"The sun just dropped into the water!" Brady yelled. "Can we have our chocolate cake now, Dad? No, I mean, Mom?"

twenty-two

Standing in front of a floor-length cheval-glass mirror in the guest bedroom of the parsonage, Jeris stepped into her wedding dress and held it together at the back. "Mom, can you zip me up?"

"Sure, honey." Her mother slowly zipped up her wedding dress.

Audra Darling stood at her left, holding the circle of flowers for Jeris's hair. "I know it's cliché, but you're the most beautiful bride I've ever seen."

"I second that." Her mother touched a long tendril at Jeris's temple. She looked at Audra Darling. "She's gorgeous, even if I am her mother."

"You're simply glowing, Jeris." Carrie, standing beside Jeris's mother, wore the bridal garter around her wrist like a bracelet, waiting to give it to Jeris. "I'm so happy for you."

"Thank you, dear ladies." Jeris looked into the full-length mirror, glancing first at the three women surrounding her, then giving her wedding dress another admiring gaze. When she and Luke had decided to get married on the banks of the water—at sunset—in the same spot where he'd proposed, she knew she didn't want a heavy, formal wedding gown. It would be too hot. And, besides, the wedding was to be casual and simple.

After several shopping trips with her mother, Audra Darling, and Carrie, she'd finally found the perfect dress. As she looked at herself from head to toe, she thought about it in Audra Darling's terms.

The dramatic white drape-neck gown has split flutter cap sleeves, a slightly fitted waistline, and an asymmetrical ruffled hem.

169

She hugged herself, running her hands along the sides of the soft crepe fabric. "It's a dream dress," she said, feeling nearly as dizzy as when Luke proposed.

"For a dream couple." Audra Darling placed the flower garland in Jeris's hair.

"For a dream wedding," her mother said.

"It *is* dreamy, isn't it? The wedding?" Jeris worked to get the flower garland just right.

"A wedding on the water," Audra Darling said. "At sunset."

Jeris's mother nodded. "With two old ladies and one young one as attendants."

Carrie handed Jeris the garter.

"And a little boy as the best man." Jeris took the garter, pulled it up her calf, then over her knee, remembering Brady's expression when Luke had told him he would be the best man. He'd belted out his expected "yippee!" And she and Luke had laughed.

"I'm so happy you and Luke got together." Audra Darling fiddled with Jeris's flutter sleeves.

Jeris nodded. "With a little help from you." She talked about Audra Darling's dinners and cooking lessons. And her prayers. "Audra Darling, you're my spiritual mother." She hugged her. "Thanks for everything you did in getting Luke and me together. I'll be eternally grateful."

Audra Darling waved her hand as if dismissing the compliment. "I did what I felt in my heart I needed to do."

Jeris hugged Carrie. "And you helped me also, Carrie. I needed to hear what you had to say about not boxing God in. I needed your prayers, too. Thanks, Carrie, for all you did."

"As the old saying goes, 'A friend in need is a friend indeed.'" Absently she touched her rounded tummy.

"I want to show my appreciation by hosting your baby shower." Jeris was thrilled for Carrie and her little one who would soon make his arrival.

Carrie smiled brilliantly.

"Audra Darling cooked dinners to get you and Luke together," Jeris's mother said, "and Carrie dispensed advice, but, hey, I provided the bride."

They all laughed, and Jeris gave her mother a hug.

"I hear the bridal march." Audra Darling ran to the door and opened it. She bowed low and thrust out her hand with a flourish. "Jeris, your groom is waiting."

"Yippee!"

~

Jeris stood on the banks of the water, encircled by Luke's arms, looking intently into his eyes, posing for a shot by the photographer. They'd said their vows and been pronounced man and wife earlier. Now the sun was setting, the guests were milling about eating the luscious hors d'oeuvres Audra Darling had made, and the photographer was giving commands to turn this way and that.

"I'm the happiest man in the world," Luke whispered to her.

"I'm the happiest woman in the world, Luke."

"No talking," the photographer said.

Feeling as if her heart would burst from happiness, she reached up and traced his jawline, her gaze taking in his every nuance.

"Hold that pose, Jeris," the photographer said. "I like it."

"I love you," Luke whispered.

"I love you, too."

"Let's have a kiss," the photographer said.

"Gladly." Luke came toward her, gazing into her eyes, and kissed her deeply.

Her heart beat its familiar trill, and the tingles started up her spine as he continued to kiss her.

"Keep it up," the photographer said.

"I'll keep this up for all eternity," Luke said.

She giggled in his arms.

"The sun is right behind your heads," the photographer said. "It'll be a perfect shot. No talking. Just keep kissing."

"If he only knew how much I'm enjoying this."

She giggled again.

"Hold still," the photographer said. *Click. Click. Click.* "Okay. I have my picture."

He didn't release her.

"I said I have my picture."

"Come up for air, Luke." Audra Darling stood a few feet away, laughing along with the rest of the crowd.

"Yes, Luke," Pastor Hughes chimed in.

Luke finally released Jeris, and the crowd applauded.

"Speech, speech!" someone called out.

He was winded from their kissing. He took a deep breath. "This lad's heart is bursting with joy."

A Letter To Our Readers

Dear Reader:

In order that we might better contribute to your reading enjoyment, we would appreciate your taking a few minutes to respond to the following questions. We welcome your comments and read each form and letter we receive. When completed, please return to the following:

Fiction Editor
Heartsong Presents
PO Box 719
Uhrichsville, Ohio 44683

1. Did you enjoy reading *The Heart of the Matter* by Kristy Dykes?
   ❑ Very much! I would like to see more books by this author!
   ❑ Moderately. I would have enjoyed it more if

   _____
   _____
   _____

2. Are you a member of **Heartsong Presents**? ❑ Yes ❑ No
   If no, where did you purchase this book? _____
   _____

3. How would you rate, on a scale from 1 (poor) to 5 (superior), the cover design? _____

4. On a scale from 1 (poor) to 10 (superior), please rate the following elements.

   ____ Heroine   ____ Plot
   ____ Hero   ____ Inspirational theme
   ____ Setting   ____ Secondary characters

5. These characters were special because? _____
_____
_____

6. How has this book inspired your life? _____
_____
_____

7. What settings would you like to see covered in future
   Heartsong Presents books? _____
_____
_____

8. What are some inspirational themes you would like to see
   treated in future books? _____
_____
_____

9. Would you be interested in reading other **Heartsong
   Presents** titles? ❏ Yes ❏ No

10. Please check your age range:
    ❏ Under 18   ❏ 18-24
    ❏ 25-34   ❏ 35-45
    ❏ 46-55   ❏ Over 55

Name _____
Occupation _____
Address _____
City, State, Zip _____